Present Laughter

A LIGHT COMEDY IN THREE ACTS

by Noël Coward

SAMUEL FRENCH, INC.
45 West 25th Street NEW YORK 10010
7623 Sunset Boulevard HOLLYWOOD 90046
LONDON *TORONTO*

ISBN 978-0-573-61425-5 Printed in U.S.A. #852

PRESENT LAUGHTER

STORY OF THE PLAY

(5 Males; 6 Females)

This latest audacious comedy by the master wit and satirist was sucessfully presented in New York at the Plymouth Theatre starring Clifton Webb. A recent revival in London surpassed its earlier triumphant run. Garry Essendine, a popular and pampered actor, is busily making preparations for an extended tour. His apartment is invaded by Daphne, a beautiful but stage-struck youngster. When his wife, his partners and his numerous admirers arrive, Garry is hard pressed to escape an embarrassing and easily misinterperted situation for both him and Daphne. With typical Coward repartee and dazzling wit, he sidesteps complications and mounting confusion. Having locked Daphne in a room, he flees his flat with his wife Liz, with whom he has been reunited. "He(Noel Coward) is still master of the quick and impudent sardonic line . . . sharp, withering and funny."—*N. Y. Times.* "It has its say with eloquence and brilliant theatrical effect."—*N. Y. Herald-Tribune.* "Sharpness and wit . . . it can be said that they grew more numerous with each succeeding act."—*N. Y. Post.*

Play by Noel Coward; staged by John C. Wilson; setting by Donald Oenslager; costumes designed by Castillo; other costumes supervised by Silvia Saal; presented by John C. Wilson at the Plymouth Theatre Tuesday Evening, October 29th, 1946.

THE CAST

DAPHNE STILLINGTON .... *Jan Sterling*
MISS ERIKSON .... *Grace Mills*
FRED .... *Aidan Turner*
MONICA REED .... *Evelyn Varden*
GARRY ESSENDINE .... *Clifton Webb*
LIZ ESSENDINE .... *Doris Dalton*
ROLAND MAULE .... *Cris Alexander*
MORRIS DIXON .... *Gordon Mills*
HUGO LYPPIATT .... *Robin Craven*
JOANNA LYPPIATT .... *Marta Linden*
LADY SALTBURN .... *Leonora Harris*

SYNOPSIS

The action passes in Garry Essendine's studio in London.

TIME: *The present.*

Act I. *Morning.*

Act II.
SCENE 1. *Evening. Three days later.*
SCENE 2. *The next morning.*

Act III. *Evening. A week later.*

Present Laughter

ACT ONE

SCENE: *The scene is* GARRY ESSENDINE'S *Studio in London.*

At down Right there is a door leading into the spare bedroom. Above this is a fireplace; in rear alcove and hall leading to the front door. Just below and on the Left of this is a staircase leading to GARRY'S *bedroom. At back of the alcove behind a screen is the entrance to the kitchen. A large window Left and below that another door leading into the office. The furnishing is comfortable, if a trifle eccentric. Down Right below the fireplace is a chair; above it a table; against the railing a small sofa. In the alcove is a bar against the Right railing, also bookshelves and miscellaneous furniture; and a screen concealing the kitchen door in rear wall. A chair Left of step leading down from the hall; a piano and a bench in front of the window; a chair against wall below piano; another chair down Left below the door. A pouffe Right Center. An armchair Center, with end table between it and the sofa which is Left Center. An end table with telephone Left of the sofa. Flowers (blue) on piano. Iris on bar; sherry glasses.*

When the Curtain rises it is about 10:30 a. m. DAPHNE STILLINGTON *comes out of the spare room down Right. She is a pretty girl of about twenty-three or four. She is wearing a man's dressing-gown and pyjamas. She wanders about until she finds the telephone and then, almost furtively, dials a number.*

DAPHNE. *(Sits on sofa)* Hallo—hallo! Cynthia darling, it's Daphne—yes—are you alone? Listen, I'm —you know where— Yes, I did— I can't go on about it now, someone might come in— If anybody rings up from home will you swear to say that I stayed with you — Darling, you promised— In that case say I'm in the bath or something— Yes, as soon as I'm dressed, in about an hour I should think—of course— I can't wait to tell you— All right. All right.— Goodbye.

(She puts down the telephone and goes over towards the kitchen door. She has nearly reached it when MISS ERIKSON *comes through it.* MISS ERIKSON *is a thin, vague-looking Swedish housekeeper. She is wearing a chintz smock, gloves and very tattered bedroom slippers. She is smoking a cigarette.)*

DAPHNE. *(A trifle nervously)* Good morning.

MISS ERIKSON. *(Crosses to Center table at Right of sofa, dusting. Betraying no surprise)* Good morning.

DAPHNE. *(Crossing to Right Center)* What time is Mr. Essendine going to be called?

MISS ERIKSON. He will ring.

DAPHNE. What time does he *usually* ring?

MISS ERIKSON. That depends what time he went to bed.

DAPHNE. *(A step Center. In a rush)* I'm afraid we were rather late last night. You see, we were at a party and Mr. Essendine very kindly said he'd drive me home, and then I found I'd forgotten my latchkey and I knew I shouldn't be able to make any of the servants hear because they sleep at the top of the house. So he said I could stay the night here so I did. *(Crosses to up Center.)*

MISS ERIKSON. *(Crossing to table Left)* If you were very late he will probably sleep until the afternoon.

DAPHNE *(Turns Right a step)* Oh dear! Couldn't you call him?

MISS ERIKSON. Alas no, we can never call him. *(Crosses to Center front of sofa.)*

DAPHNE. Well, do you think I could have some coffee or orange juice or something?

MISS ERIKSON. I will see. *(As she goes out)* Fred! ! ! *(She goes out through the kitchen door.)*

(DAPHNE *crosses to mirror Right. After a few moments* FRED *enters from kitchen.* FRED *is* GARRY'S *valet. He is smartly dressed and wears a black alpaca coat.)*

DAPHNE. Good morning.

FRED. *(Crossing Down Center)* Good morning.

DAPHNE. Have *you* any idea what time Mr. Essendine will wake up?

FRED. Might be any time, he didn't leave no note.

DAPHNE. *(Crossing Down Right)* Couldn't you call him? It's nearly eleven o'clock.

FRED. *(A step down)* The whole place goes up in smoke if we wake him by accident, let alone call 'im.

DAPHNE. Well, do you think I could have some breakfast?

FRED. What would you fancy?

DAPHNE. Coffee, please, and some orange juice.

FRED. Rightyo. *(Exits to kitchen.)*

(MONICA REED, GARRY'S *secretary, comes in from the hall.* DAPHNE *rolls up pajama leg at pouffe.* MONICA *is in her hat and coat and carries a bundle of letters. She is a pleasant, rather austere woman in the early forties.)*

DAPHNE. Good morning.

MONICA. *(Crossing Down Left of pouffe)* —Good morning. I am Mr. Essendine's secretary. Is there anything I can do for you?

DAPHNE. Well, I'm afraid it's rather awkward—you see, Mr. Essendine drove me home last night from a party and I idiotically forgot my latchkey, and so he very sweetly said I could stay here—in the spare room.

MONICA. *(Crossing to table Left)* I hope you were warm enough.

DAPHNE. Oh yes, quite, thank you.

MONICA. It's liable to be a bit nippy in the spare room.

DAPHNE. I kept the heater on.

MONICA. Very sensible.

DAPHNE. *(Crossing to Right Center)* And now I was wondering if somebody could tell Mr. Essendine that I'm—here.

MONICA. I expect he'll remember when he wakes up.

DAPHNE. Have you any idea when that will be?

MONICA. I'm afraid not. If he didn't leave any special time to be called he might sleep on indefinitely.

DAPHNE. I don't want to go away without saying goodbye and thanking him.

(After MONICA'S *look,* DAPHNE *sits pouffe. Pause.)*

MONICA. *(Crossing to Center)* If I were you I should have some breakfast and dress and if he isn't awake by then you can leave a message for him. Have you asked for any breakfast?

DAPHNE. Yes, I think the man's bringing it.

MONICA. *(Crossing to* DAPHNE) Have you known Mr. Essendine long?

DAPHNE. Well, no, not exactly— I mean of course I've *known him* for ages. I think he's wonderful, but we actually only *met* last night for the first time.

MONICA. *(Quizzically)* I see.

DAPHNE. I think he's even more charming off the stage than on, don't you?

MONICA. *(With a slight smile)* I can never quite make up my mind.

DAPHNE. Have you been with him for a long while?

MONICA. Just on seventeen years.

DAPHNE. *(Enthusiastically)* How wonderful! I expect you know him better than anybody.

MONICA. *(Crosses to chair Center and sits)* Less intimately than some, better than most.

DAPHNE. *(Swings around)* Is he happy, do you think? I mean really happy?

MONICA. I don't believe I've ever asked him.

DAPHNE. He has a sad look in his eyes every now and then.

MONICA. Oh, you noticed that, did you?

DAPHNE. We talked for hours last night. He told me all about his early struggles.

MONICA. Did he by any chance mention that Life was passing him by?

DAPHNE. I think he did say something like that.

MONICA. Oh dear!

DAPHNE. Why?

MONICA. I only wondered.

DAPHNE. You've no idea how I envy you, working for him, but then I expect everybody does. It must be absolute heaven.

MONICA. It's certainly not dull.

(Pause.)

DAPHNE. *(Rise)* I hope you don't think it's awful of me spending the night— I mean it does look rather bad, doesn't it?

MONICA. *(Rise)* Well really, Miss—Miss—?

DAPHNE. Stillington, Daphne Stillington.

MONICA. *(Crossing to table Left)* Miss Stillington— it's hardly my business, is it?

DAPHNE. No, I suppose not, but I wouldn't like you to think—

MONICA. Seventeen years is a long time, Miss Stillington. I gave up that sort of thinking in the spring of Nineteen Thirty-three—

DAPHNE. Oh, I see.

(FRED *comes out of the kitchen with a tray of orange juice, coffee and toast.)*

FRED. *(Crossing Left Center)* Will you 'ave it in here, Miss, or in the bedroom?

DAPHNE. *(Sits pouffe)* Here, please.

MONICA. *(Crossing to Center)* I think it would really be more comfortable for you in the bedroom. (FRED *exits down Right)* The studio becomes rather active round about eleven. People call, you know, and the telephone rings— *(Takes coat off.* DAPHNE *rises. Pushing* DAPHNE *to door down Right)* I'll let you know the minute he wakes up.

DAPHNE. Thank you so much. (MONICA *crosses to Center.* FRED *enters, whistling.)*

MONICA. Fred, is there any soap in that bathroom?

FRED. *(Crossing to Center)* Yes, but the tap's a bit funny. You 'ave to go on turning it till Kingdom come. *(DOORBELL rings.)*

MONICA. *(Crossing to Center)* Did you tell her?

FRED. *(Goes to front door)* She'll find out for herself.

MONICA. *(Crossing to table Left)* You'd better send Miss Erikson in to her.

FRED. *(Returns with a box)* She's gone to the grocers, but I'll tell 'er when she comes back.

MONICA. Fred! Were you here last night?

FRED. No. She's news to me.

MONICA. If he hasn't rung by twelve we'd better wake him.

FRED. *(Starts out)* Well, if the balloon goes up don't blame me.

(At this moment GARRY ESSENDINE *appears at the top of the stairs. He is in his pajamas and his hair is tousled.)*

GARRY. *(Furiously)* I suppose it's of no interest to any of you that I have been awakened from a deep sleep by everybody screaming like banshees. What's going on?

MONICA. I've been talking to Miss Stillington.

GARRY. Who the hell is Miss Stillington?

MONICA. She's in the spare room.

GARRY. *(Coming down)* I didn't ask you where she was, I asked you who she was?

MONICA. We might look her up in the telephone book.

FRED. She forgot her latchkey if you know what I mean.

GARRY. *(Crossing down Center)* Go away, Fred, and get me some coffee.

FRED. *(Crossing to step Center)* Rightyo.

GARRY. And don't say rightyo.

FRED. Very good, sir. *(He goes to kitchen.)*

MONICA. You met her at a party and brought her home here and told her about your early struggles, and she stayed the night.

GARRY. *(Sits sofa)* She's a darling. I remember now. I'm mad about her. What did you say her name was?

MONICA. Stillington. Daphne Stillington.

GARRY. I knew it was Daphne, but I hadn't the faintest idea it was Stillington. How did she look to you?

MONICA. Restive.

GARRY. Poor sweet, I hope you were nice to her. Has anybody given her anything to eat?

MONICA. Fred took her some coffee and orange juice.

GARRY. What's she doing now?

MONICA. I don't know, drinking it, I suppose.

GARRY. It's awful, isn't it? What are we to do?

MONICA. She wants to say goodbye to you and to thank you.

GARRY. Whatever for?

MONICA. That, Garry dear, I am in no position to say.

GARRY. *(Rises; crosses to Center)* Why didn't you tell her to dress quietly like a mouse and go home? You know perfectly well it's agony here in the morning with everybody banging about.

MONICA. You might have thought of that before you asked her to stay the night.

GARRY. She had to stay the night. She'd lost her key.

MONICA. The sooner we turn that spare room into a library the better. *(Smiling.)*

GARRY. She's probably sobbing her heart out.

MONICA. Why don't you go and see?

GARRY. Lend me a comb and I will.

MONICA. *(Taking a comb out of her bag)* Here.

GARRY. *(Taking mirror from Center table)* Good God, I look ninety-eight.

MONICA. Never mind.

GARRY. I bet some day I'll be bald as a coot, and then you'll be sorry.

MONICA. On the contrary I shall be delighted. There will be fewer eager young debutantes willing to lose their latchkeys for you when you've got a toupee perched on the top of your head, and life will be a great deal simpler.

GARRY. *(Crossing to* MONICA. *Thoughtfully)* I shall never wear a toupee, Monica, however bald I get. Perhaps on the stage I might have a little front piece, but in life, never! I intend to grow old with distinction. *(Sits on sofa.)*

MONICA. *(Doing mail)* Well, I'm sure that will be a great relief to all of us.

GARRY. Here's your sordid little comb.

MONICA. *(Taking it and putting it back in her bag)* Now do go and do a nice goodbye scene, there's a dear, and get rid of her as quickly as possible.

(Pause.)

GARRY. *(Rises; crosses to Center)* I haven't done my exercises yet.

MONICA. You can do those after she's gone.

GARRY. *(Exercising)* I can't go into that spare room in my pajamas, it's like an icebox.

MONICA. The heater's on. It's been on all night.

GARRY. Very extravagant.

DAPHNE. *(Comes out of the room, Right)* Garry.

GARRY. Darling!

DAPHNE. I thought I heard your voice.

MONICA. If you want me I shall be in the office, Garry.

GARRY. *(Crossing to sofa. With great politeness)* Thank you, Monica.

MONICA. *(Crossing Down Left)* And don't forget that at one sharp Morris is coming to discuss what understudies you are going to take to Africa.

GARRY. No, Monica.

MONICA. And that at twelve-thirty you have given an appointment to a Mr. Roland Maule.

GARRY. I shall remember.

MONICA. I'm so glad. *(Crossing to door Left)* Goodbye Miss Stillington. I do hope we shall meet again.

DAPHNE. Goodbye. *(*MONICA *goes out into the office and shuts the door firmly.* DAPHNE *runs to* GARRY *and flings her arms around him. Burying her face in his shoulder.)* Garry! Oh Garry!

GARRY. Darling.

DAPHNE. *(Sits sofa)* I'm ridiculously happy.

GARRY. *(Sits Left of her)* I'm so glad, darling.

DAPHNE. Are you?

GARRY. Happy?

DAPHNE. *(Taking his hand)* Yes.

GARRY. *(Gently withdrawing his hand and turning away)* There's something awfully sad about happiness, isn't there?

DAPHNE. What a funny thing to say.

GARRY. It wasn't meant to be funny.

DAPHNE. *(Arms around his neck)* I've been in love with you for such a long time.

GARRY. *(Takes her arms down)* Don't—don't say that.

DAPHNE. Why? What's the matter?

GARRY. Don't love me too much, Daphne! Promise me you won't. You'll only be unhappy. No good can come of loving anyone like me— I'm not worthy of it, really I'm not.

DAPHNE. You're more worthy of it than anybody in the whole world.

GARRY. Foolish child.

DAPHNE. I'm not a child. I'm twenty-one.

GARRY. *(Smilingly)* Twenty-one! If only I were younger—if only you were older—

DAPHNE. What does age matter when people love each other?

GARRY. I wonder how tragically often that has been said.

DAPHNE. It's true.

GARRY. Look at me, Daphne. Look at me kindly, clearly and honestly—look at the lines on my face—look at my eyes!

DAPHNE. You're not so very old.

GARRY. *(With a touch of asperity)* I didn't say I was so very old, Daphne, I merely said look at me. As a matter of fact, I'm only just—forty.

DAPHNE. What's forty?

GARRY. Too old for twenty-one.

DAPHNE. You mean you don't love me?

GARRY. I don't mean any such thing.

DAPHNE. Do you love me? Say it—do you?

GARRY. Of course I do.

DAPHNE. Say it!

GARRY. I love you, Daphne.

DAPHNE. *(Arms around neck)* Oh, darling—

GARRY. *(Taking both her hands off)* But this is goodbye!

DAPHNE. *(Aghast)* Goodbye? But Garry—

GARRY. It must be. It's inevitable. Not for my sake, my dear, but for yours. Last night—suddenly—a spark was struck! The flame burned brightly—that was happiness!—something to be remembered always—

DAPHNE. *(Weeping)* You're different this morning—you don't love me—you didn't mean any of the things you said last night.

GARRY. Youth never understands. That's what's so

absolutely awful about Youth—it never, never understands. *(Rises; crosses Left.)*

DAPHNE. *(With spirit)* I don't know what you're talking about.

GARRY. *(Back of Left end of sofa)* Listen to me, my dearest. You're not in love with me—the real me. You're in love with an illusion, the illusion that I gave you when you saw me on the stage. Last night I ran the risk of breaking that dear young illusion for ever—but I didn't— It's still there. I can see it in your eyes but never again—never never again—moments like last night—that's all I can dare to hope for now—that's why I'm so lonely sometimes, so desperately lonely, but I have learned one bitter lesson in my life and that lesson is to be able to say goodbye—

DAPHNE. But Garry—

GARRY. Let me go on— Ssh!

"We meet not as we parted
We feel more than all may see;
My bosom is heavy-hearted
And thine full of doubt for me.
One moment has bound the free."

(Crosses front of sofa.)

DAPHNE. But, Garry—

GARRY. Quiet!

"That moment has gone forever,
Like lightning that flashed and died,
Like a snowflake upon the river,
Like a sunbeam upon the tide,
Which the dark shadows hide—"

(Stops front table Left) There now, that was Shelley. Don't you think it's beautiful?

DAPHNE. Yes, but—

GARRY. *(Right of chair Center)* There was nothing Shelley didn't know about love, not a thing! All the sadness, all the joy, all the unbearable pain—

DAPHNE. Yes—but I don't see why love should be so miserable.

GARRY. *(Kneeling on Center chair. Laughing bitterly)* That's because you're young, my sweet—young and eager and greedy for life— *(Tenderly putting his arms around her. Sitting Right of her.)*

DAPHNE. You said last night that now that you had found me you would never let me go.

GARRY. That was perfectly true. I shall never let you go. You shall be here in my heart forever.

DAPHNE. *(Crying)* Oh, Garry—

GARRY. Don't cry—please, please don't cry— I can't bear it—cover up, cover up. *(Fixes* DAPHNE'S *dressing gown.)*

DAPHNE. *(Clinging to him)* How can you say that I'm only in love with an illusion and not the real you at all—

GARRY. Because it's true.

DAPHNE. It isn't—it isn't—it was the real you last night, you weren't on the stage—you weren't acting—

GARRY. I'm always acting—watching myself go by—that's what's so horrible.

DAPHNE. I could help you if only you'd let me.

GARRY. *(Very quietly)* Listen, my dear. It isn't that I don't love you, I do.

DAPHNE. Oh, Garry. *(She throws her arms around him.)*

GARRY. *(Rises; crosses to Center)* But my life is not my own— I belong to my work. In two weeks' time I am going away to Africa with a repertory of six plays—do you understand what that means? The work, the drudgery, the nerve strain? When I come back, *if* I come back, I shall look at you again and I shall know—in the first glance—whether you have waited for me or not—please come here now and kiss me— *(She runs to him)* once, just once and then go—

DAPHNE. *(Running to him)* Oh Garry—oh darling—

GARRY. Au revoir, my sweet—not goodbye—just au revoir.

(Starts walking her to door Right. He embraces her;

then pats her behind and releases her. She looks at him uncertainly for a moment and then goes weeping into the bedroom and shuts the door. FRED *comes out of the kitchen with a breakfast tray.* GARRY *crosses Left.)*

FRED. Do you want your coffee here or upstairs?
GARRY. Anywhere—put it anywhere.

(DOORBELL rings.)

FRED. I'd have brought it in before but I 'eard all the weeping and wailing going on and I thought I'd better wait.

(TELEPHONE rings.)

GARRY. Put the tray down, Fred, and go away.
FRED. *(Whistles)* Rightyo.

(ERIKSON *enters from kitchen; calls,* "FRED," *answers door and gets package and exits to kitchen.* FRED *puts the tray front of chair Center and pours coffee.* MONICA *comes out of the office with opened letters. The TELEPHONE rings.)*

GARRY. *(Sits chair Center. Irritably)* My God, there's no peace—no peace anywhere— (FRED *whistles)* Why is that phone ringing in the room.
MONICA. *(Going to the telephone)* I switched the telephone in here because we've got to go through the mail and I can't keep darting in and out of the office all the time.
GARRY. Will you stop that repulsive whistling.

(FRED *exits whistling to kitchen.)*

MONICA. *(At telephone)* Hallo—hallo—Mr. Essendine's secretary speaking—no I'm afraid he's not available at the moment. (GARRY *dunks toast)* Well, he's very busy just now, I think perhaps it would be better if you wrote— No, I'm sorry, that's quite impossible— (MISS ERIKSON *enters and crosses Down Center)* Very well—not at all— Goodbye. *(She hangs up crosses to chair down Left; pulls up chair and sits.)*

MISS ERIKSON. Fred said I was to go and speak to the young lady.

GARRY. Very well, Miss Erikson.

MISS ERIKSON. What shall I say to her?

GARRY. I really don't know.

MISS ERIKSON. I have been to the grocer's and—

GARRY. That's as good an opening gambit as any.

MONICA. *(Crosses to sofa)* Just see that she has everything she wants, Miss Erikson, and turn on a bath for her.

MISS ERIKSON. Alas, no, that I cannot do, the tap makes no water.

GARRY. Do the best you can.

MISS ERIKSON. I will try. *(She goes into the bedroom, Right.)*

GARRY. That's a good girl.

MONICA. *(Sits sofa)* There's nothing much this morning. I'll go through them quickly.

GARRY. The coffee tastes of curry powder.

MONICA. Never mind.

GARRY. I wish I had a French chef instead of a Scandinavian spiritualist.

MONICA. You could never get rid of Miss Erikson, she worships you.

GARRY. Everybody worships me, it's nauseating.

MONICA. There's hell to pay if they don't.

GARRY. What's that blue letter?

MONICA. Sylvia Laurie, she says she must see you before you go away.

GARRY. *(Smells letter)* Well, she can't.

MONICA. Here's one from that young man you forced to go to the Slade School; he's very *unhappy.*

GARRY. I didn't force him, he asked me for my advice and I gave it to him.

MONICA. Well, he says he's hedged in by obsolete conventions, that his inspiration's withered and that it's all your fault. Here, read the rest of it yourself. *(Hands him letter.)*

GARRY. He's a damn fool. I knew it the moment I clapped eyes on him.

MONICA. In that case it would have been wiser not to have let him think that you minded so passionately about his career.

GARRY. What the hell is the matter with the light in the room? If people don't want my advice why the hell do they come and badger me?

MONICA. Here's a postcard I can't make head or tail of.

GARRY. *(Snatches card from* MONICA. *Turning it round in his hands)* It's from Brazil.

MONICA. I know, it says so on the stamp.

GARRY. *(Reading)* I've done what you said and it's nearly finished. I can't read the signature, it looks like Pickett.

MONICA. Can you remember anyone called Pickett that you sent to Brazil to finish something?

GARRY. *(Giving her the postcard)* Tear it up, people should write legibly or not at all.

MONICA. Not at all would be lovely. *(Enter* ERIKSON *Right and crosses to Center)* Is Miss Stillington nearly dressed?

MISS ERIKSON. Yes, but she is crying which makes her slow.

GARRY. Crying!

MISS ERIKSON. The tap is on the blink.

MONICA. You'd better go upstairs, Garry.

GARRY. *(Rises; starts up)* Tell Fred.

MONICA. *(Rises; crosses to table Left)* Tell Fred Mr. Essendine wants his bath, Miss Erikson.

MISS ERIKSON. I will tell him. Fred! Fred! (MISS ERIKSON *goes off to kitchen.)*

GARRY. *(Rises; crosses to Center)* You'd better come up too, we can do the rest of the letters up there.

MONICA. There are only two more. An invitation from Gertrude Lovat. She's giving a coming-out dance for that pimply-looking daughter of hers—

GARRY. Polite refusal.

MONICA. And rather a complicated letter from some Boy Scouts.

GARRY. *(On platform)* To hell with them.

MONICA. Apparently you're a patron of their dramatic club and they're giving a performance of "Laughter in Heaven" and want you to send them a message.

GARRY. *(Going upstairs)* All right—send them one.

MONICA. What shall I say?

GARRY. *(Patiently)* Monica dear, don't tell me that you have arrived at the age of eighty-nine and are unable to send a message. (GARRY *goes off)* Boy Scouts, send them some matches.

(DOORBELL rings. FRED *comes on again and collects the breakfast tray and exits to kitchen. The TELEPHONE rings.* MONICA *goes to answer it.* MISS ERIKSON *goes to front door;* FRED *enters and goes upstairs.)*

MONICA. *(At telephone)* Hallo—Oh, Hugo—yes, he's in but he's just gone to have his bath— Today? I thought you weren't going until the end of the week—Yes, of course— He's not lunching until half-past—All right, I'll tell him— (MONICA *hangs up the telephone.)*

(LIZ's *voice is heard saying; "Hallo Miss Erikson—is everybody in" After a moment she comes in.* MISS ERIKSON *follows her and goes off again.* LIZ *is a charming-looking woman in the thirties. She is well dressed but not elaborate. She carries two parcels.)*

LIZ *(Crosses Down Center)* Good morning, Monica dear.

MONICA. *(Crossing to* LIZ) Liz: We thought you weren't coming back until tonight.

LIZ. I came over by plane, loaded with gifts like an Eastern potentate. Here's one for you.

MONICA. *(Taking the parcel that* LIZ *gives her)* How lovely!

LIZ. It's a bottle of perfume and very expensive.

MONICA. *(Crosses to sofa)* Thanks ever so much, Liz, you're a darling.

LIZ. What's God up to?

MONICA. In the bath.

LIZ. I've brought him a dressing-gown.

MONICA. *(Sits sofa)* How thoughtful—he's only got eighteen.

LIZ. *(Crossing to piano)* Don't be acid, Monica, you know he loves peacocking about in something new. It's nice and thin and highly suitable for Africa.

MONICA. This looks wonderful, Liz. I won't open it until I get home.

LIZ. *(She puts the other parcel on the piano and takes off her hat and coat)* Miss Erikson looked more peculiar than ever this morning. Is her spiritualism getting worse? *(Crosses to Center.)*

MONICA. She got in touch with a dead friend at a seance on Sunday night, and all he said was "No, no, no" and "Christmas Day!" It upset her very much. *(The TELEPHONE rings.* LIZ *puts gloves on Right table)* That damned thing never stops. "Hallo—hallo—Morris? —No, he's in the bath— Liz is here if you want to talk to her—yes, she's just arrived—" Here, Liz. (MONICA *gives* LIZ *the telephone and, while she's talking, opens her present.)*

LIZ. *(Crosses to sofa and sits Left end. At telephone)* Good morning, dear— No—on the plane— Yes, I saw the play twice— We shall have to alter the end for England, but I talked to the author and he didn't seem to mind what happened as long as Garry played it—

No, I'm lunching out but I'll come to the office directly afterwards if you like— All right. Goodbye. *(She hangs up.)*

(FRED *comes down the stairs whistling.)*

LIZ. Hallo, Fred—how's everything?
FRED. Bit of a lash up, Miss, as usual.
LIZ. *(Rise: crossing to Center)* Do you think I could have a cup of coffee— I feel a sinking.
FRED. Rightyo, Miss. *(Goes off through the kitchen door.)*
MONICA. Bring me one too, Fred.
FRED. Rightyo.
LIZ. *(Crossing to Center)* It's very resolute of Fred to go on calling me, Miss, isn't it?
MONICA. *(Crossing front of sofa)* I think he has sort of an idea that when you gave up being Garry's wife you automatically reverted to maidenhood.
LIZ. *(Starts Up Center)* It's a very pretty thought.

(DAPHNE *comes out of the spare room in an evening dress and cloak. She is no longer crying but looks depressed. She jumps slightly on seeing* LIZ.)

DAPHNE. *(Front of pouffe)* Oh! I beg your pardon.
MONICA. I'm so awfully sorry about the bath, Miss Stillington.
DAPHNE. It didn't matter a bit.
MONICA. This is *Mrs.* Essendine—Miss Stillington.
DAPHNE. Oh!
LIZ. *(Amiably)* How do you do?
DAPHNE. *(Shattered)* Mrs. Essendine! Do you mean — I mean— Are you Garry's wife?
LIZ. Yes.
DAPHNE. Oh— I thought he was divorced.
LIZ. We never quite got around to it.
DAPHNE. *(Drops bag)* Oh, I see.
LIZ. *(Picks up her bag. Crosses to* DAPHNE) But

please don't look agitated— I upped and left him years ago.

MONICA. *(A trifle wickedly)* Miss Stillington lost her key last night and so she slept in the spare room.

LIZ. *(To* DAPHNE) You poor dear, you must be absolutely congealed.

DAPHNE. Do you think I could get a taxi?

MONICA. *(Crossing to table Left)* I'll ring for one.

LIZ. No, don't do that, my car's downstairs, it can take you wherever you want to go. *(Breaks Center.)*

(MONICA *goes to window; then crosses back of sofa.)*

DAPHNE. It's most awfully kind of you.

LIZ. Not at all, the chauffeur's got bright red hair and his name's Frobisher—you can't miss him.

DAPHNE. *(Crosses to* LIZ) Thank you very much indeed—you're sure it's not inconvenient?

(MONICA *crosses Left to back of sofa.)*

LIZ. *(Briskly)* Not in the least— Just tell him to come straight back here after he's dropped you.

(MONICA *crosses up Center on platform.)*

DAPHNE. *(Crosses and shakes hands with* LIZ. *Still floundering)* Oh—yes—of course I will—thank you again—goodbye.

LIZ. Goodbye— I do hope you haven't caught cold.

DAPHNE. *(Crosses to hall. Laughing nervously)* No, I don't think so—goodbye.

MONICA. I'll see you out.

DAPHNE. *(Goes out front door)* Please don't trouble—

(LIZ *crosses to table Left.* FRED *comes in with two cups of coffee.)*

MONICA. *(Sees* DAPHNE *out)* It's no trouble at all.
FRED. *(Crosses to table Left)* Would you like anything with it, Miss?
LIZ. No, thank you, Fred, just the coffee.
FRED. I'll tell his Nibs you're here— I don't think he knows.
LIZ. Thank you, Fred. (FRED *bounds upstairs.)*
MONICA. *(Entering from hall)* Well!
LIZ. Has that been going on long, or is it new?
MONICA. *(Crossing front of sofa to* LIZ) Quite new — I found it wandering about in Garry's pyjamas.
LIZ. *(Hands* MONICA *coffee)* Poor little thing, how awful for her to be faced with me like that, you ought to have pretended I was someone else.
MONICA. *(Sits Right end of sofa)* Serve her right, she ought to be ashamed of herself.
LIZ. She seemed to be what is known as a "lady." It's all very odd, isn't it- *(Sits Left of* MONICA.)
MONICA. That type's particularly idiotic and the woods are full of them, they go shambling about London without hats and making asses of themselves.
LIZ. Very discouraging.
MONICA. I don't mind if only they'd leave Garry alone, it makes the mornings so complicated, Liz.
LIZ. He's not nearly as flamboyant as he pretends to be, he's just incapable of saying "no" or "goodbye."
MONICA. He *says* "goodbye" often enough, but he always manages to give the impression that he doesn't really mean it.
LIZ. I'll have to go at him, after all, it's high time he relaxed.
MONICA. If you think a *big* scene's necessary we can get Morris and Hugo too, and have a real rouser the night before he sails.
LIZ. Morris is awfully hysterical these days and Hugo's not nearly so reliable since he married Joanna.
MONICA. *(Puts cup on table Right)* Do you like her? Joanna?

LIZ. She's a lovely creature, but tricky. Yes, I think I like her all right.

MONICA. *(Rises, crosses to Center)* I don't.

LIZ. You never would, darling, she's not your cup of tea at all.

GARRY. *(In morning clothes, comes downstairs)* Who isn't?

(MONICA *sits chair Center.)*

LIZ. Joanna.

GARRY. She's not bad, a bit predatory perhaps, but then as far as I can see everybody's predatory—everybody stalks their game as far as I can see.

LIZ. I shall give it up for Lent.

GARRY. *(Crossing back of sofa. Kissing her absently)* Good morning, darling, where's my present?

LIZ. On the piano.

GARRY. *(Crosses to piano)* It's not another one of those damn glass horses, is it?

LIZ. No, it's a dressing gown for Africa.

GARRY. *(Opening it)* Oh, Liz, how wonderful! Just what I wanted— *(He shakes it out)* It's absolutely charming—thank you, darling, I'm mad about it. *(Crosses Down Right. Puts it on and looks at it in the glass)* It really is perfect taste, the best sort of Colonial propaganda! *(Stands on pouffe)* Say something about it, Monica.

MONICA. I'm speechless.

LIZ. Go away then, Monica, I must talk to Garry before *Morris* gets here, it's important.

MONICA. *(Rises; crosses to Center)* You'd better hurry, Mr. Maule will be here in a minute.

GARRY. Who's he?

MONICA. You know perfectly well, he's the young man who wrote that mad play half in verse and caught you on the telephone, and you were so busy being attractive and unspoiled by your great success that you promised him an appointment.

GARRY. I can't see him—you ought to protect me from things like that.

MONICA. You must see him, he's coming all the way from Uckfield and it serves you right for snatching the telephone when I wasn't looking.

GARRY. I've noticed a great change in you lately, Monica. I don't know whether it's because you've given up cramming yourself with potatoes or what it is, but you're geting nastier with every day that passes. Go away.

MONICA. *(Crossing Left. Gathering up her bottle of scent from table. Puts coffee cup on table Left)* I'm going. I shall be in the office if you want me.

GARRY. *(Crosses and puts robe on piano)* Of course you'll be in the office, spinning awful plots and intrigues against me.

MONICA. I will if I can think of any. *(Goes into the office.)*

GARRY. *(Shouting after her)* Shut the telephone off.

MONICA. *(Off)* All right.

GARRY. Now then, tell me all about your trip and everything. What did you think of the play?

LIZ. It was wonderful.

GARRY. That's good?

LIZ. Yes, very. It's a perfect part for you. We shall have to change it, a bit, but the author's quite willing to let us do what we like as long as you play it.

GARRY. How right!

LIZ. *(Crosses to table Left and lights a cigarette)* Now then I want to talk to you about something.

GARRY. I don't like that tone at all. What's on your mind?

LIZ. Don't you think it's time you started to relax?

GARRY. I don't know what you're talking about.

LIZ. Who was that poor little creature I saw here this morning in evening dress?

GARRY. *(Crossing to chair Center)* She'd lost her latchkey.

LIZ. They often do.

GARRY. Now listen to me, Liz—

LIZ. You're over forty, you know.

GARRY. Only just.

LIZ. And in my humble opinion all this casual scampering about is rather undignified.

GARRY. *(Sits chair Center)* Scampering indeed! You have a genius for putting things unpleasantly.

LIZ. *(Crossing to pouffe)* Don't misunderstand me, I'm not taking a moral view, I gave that up as hopeless years ago.

GARRY. It's all very fine for you to come roaring back from Paris where you've been up to God knows what, and start to bully me—

LIZ. I'm not bullying you.

GARRY. Yes, you are. You're sitting smug as be damned on an awful little cloud and blowing down on me.

LIZ. Don't bluster.

GARRY. Who left my bed and board—deserted me—left me a prey to everybody? Answer me that!

LIZ. I did, thank God.

GARRY. Well then.

LIZ. Would you have liked me to have stayed?

GARRY. Certainly not, you drove me mad.

LIZ. *(Crossing back of sofa)* Well, stop shilly-shallying about then and pay attention.

GARRY. This, to date, is the most irritating morning of my life.

LIZ. You have reached a moment in life when a little restraint would be becoming.

GARRY. La-de-da.

LIZ. You are no longer a debonair, irresponsible juvenile. You are an eminent man advancing, with every sign of reluctance, into middle age.

GARRY. May God forgive you.

LIZ. *(Crossing back of sofa to front)* Never mind about that. We all know about your irresistible fascination. We've watched it going on *monotonously* for twenty years.

GARRY. I met you for the first time exactly eleven

years ago next August, and you were wearing a very silly hat.

LIZ. Will you be serious! Your behavior naturally affects all of us. Morris, Hugo, Monica and me. You're responsible for us and we're responsible for you. *(Sits sofa)* Just try *not* to be so devastatingly charming to people for a little. Think what fun it would be to be *un*attractive for a minute or two. Why, you might take to it like a duck to water.

GARRY. *(Rises, crosses and sits on sofa)* Dear Liz. You really are very sweet.

LIZ. *(Crossly)* Oh dear, I might just as well have been talking Chinese.

(Pause.)

GARRY. I admit I'm a trifle reckless every now and then, but I really don't do much harm to anybody.

LIZ. You do harm to yourself and to the few, the very few, who really mind about you.

GARRY. I suppose you've discussed all this with Monica and Morris and Hugo?

LIZ. I haven't yet, but I will unless I see some sign of improvement.

GARRY. *(Rises; crossing Right)* Blackmail, hey?

LIZ. You know how you hate it when we all make a concerted pounce.

GARRY. *(Crossing to chair Center. With exasperation, walking about)* The thing that astonishes me in life is people's arrogance! It's fantastic. Look at you all! Gossiping in corners, whispering behind your fans, telling me what to do and what not to do. It's downright sauce, that's what it is. What happens if I relax my loving hold on any of you for a minute?— Disaster! I happen to go to New York to play a three months' season. Hugo immediately gets pneumonia, goes to Biarritz to recover, meets Joanna and marries her! I go away for a brief holiday in the south of France, and when I come back what do I find? You and Morris between you had bought the dullest Hungarian play ever written and produced it with Phoebe Lucas in the leading part. Phoebe Lucas, playing a glamorous courtesan with about as much sex appeal as a finnan haddie! How long did it run? One week! And that was only because the press said it was lascivious.

LIZ. Isn't all this a little beside the point?

GARRY. Certainly not. Twenty years ago Hugo put all his money into that lousy play, "The Lost Cavalier." And who played it for eighteen months to capacity with extra matinees? I did. And who started his whole career as a producer in that play? Morris!

LIZ. I wish you'd stop asking questions and answering them yourself, it's making me giddy.

GARRY. *(Crossing Down Center)* Where would they have been without me? Where would Monica be now if I hadn't snatched her away from that sinister old aunt of hers and given her a job?

LIZ. *With* the sinister old aunt.

GARRY. And you! Dear! *You!* One of the most depressing, melancholy actresses on the English stage. Where would you be if I hadn't forced you to give up acting and start writing?

LIZ. Acting.

GARRY. Good God! I even had to marry you to do it.

LIZ. Yes, and a fine gesture that turned out to be.

GARRY. *(Crossing to Center)* You adored me, you know you did.

LIZ. I still do, dear. You're so chivalrous, rubbing it in how dependent we all are on you for every breath we take.

GARRY. I didn't say that. *(Stands on pouffe.)*

LIZ. You're just as dependent on us anyway, now. We stop you being extravagant and buying houses every five minutes. We stopped you in the nick of time, from playing Peer Gynt.

GARRY. I still maintain I should have been magnificent as Peer Gynt.

LIZ. Above all, we stop you from overacting.

GARRY. You have now gone too far, Liz, I think you had better go away somewhere.

LIZ. I've only just come back.

GARRY. *(Shouting)* Monica!— Monica! Come here at once.

MONICA. *(Entering)* What on earth's the matter?

GARRY. *(Crossing to Center)* Have you or have you not seen me overact?

MONICA. Frequently.

GARRY. *(Crosses and sits chair Center)* It's a conspiracy!— I knew it!

MONICA. As a matter of fact you're overacting now. *(She goes off Left.)*

GARRY. Very well— I give in—everybody's against me—it doesn't matter about me—oh no— I'm only the breadwinner. It doesn't matter how much I'm wounded and insulted! It doesn't matter that my timorous belief in myself should be subtly undermined.

LIZ. Your belief in yourself is about as timorous as Napoleon's.

GARRY. And look what happened to him, poor chap. He died forsaken and alone on a lousy little island all surrounded by water.

LIZ. Islands have that in common.

GARRY. You're trying to be funny now because you're ashamed. I doubt if any of you would care a fig if I were exiled forever tomorrow. You'd probably be delighted. I expect that's why I'm being *forced* to go to Africa.

LIZ. You're longing to go and you know it. But oh, darling, do be careful when you're there, and don't go having affairs with everybody and showing off. Now then, about Morris. I want you to concentrate for a minute.

GARRY. How can I concentrate? *(Rises; crosses to Center)* You come here and say the most awful things to me, tear the heart out of me and jump up and down on it and then say calmly— "Now then about Morris" as though you'd been discussing the weather. *(Exasperated)* What about Morris? What's wrong?

LIZ. *(She motions him to sofa)* I'm very worried. I think you'll have to do a little of your famous finger-wagging. It's—it's Joanna.

GARRY. Joanna? *(Crosses and sits Right of her.)*

LIZ. Morris is in love with her.

GARRY. How do you know?

LIZ. Everybody's talking about it. I don't know how far it's gone, or any details, but I do know that if it's true something ought to be done about it and at once.

GARRY. Does Hugo suspect anything?

LIZ. I don't think so, but then he never would, would he? Until it was shoved under his nose.

GARRY. He ought never to have married that stereotyped diamond-studded siren. I always said it was a grave mistake.

LIZ. I don't think she's as stereotyped as all that, but she's dangerous all right.

GARRY. *(Getting up and walking about)* Oh God, it's too tiresome, really it is—it'll upset all my plans for Africa.

LIZ. If Hugo finds out it might bust up everything.

GARRY. It might stop the whole trip. What *are* we to do, Liz? *(DOORBELL rings)* There's that beastly young man from Uckfield and here am I trembling like a leaf. I can't face him, I can't!

LIZ. You've got to if you promised.

GARRY. *(Rises; crosses to Center)* My life is one long torment and nobody even remotely cares.

LIZ. It might not be the young man at all, it might be Morris.

(DOORBELL rings.)

GARRY. To hell with Morris. To hell with everybody.

LIZ. *(Crosses to* GARRY*)* Don't be idiotic.

GARRY. It isn't Morris. He isn't coming until one o'clock.

LIZ. You've got to find out how much truth there is in this Joanna business. *(Crossing to piano, picks up her hat)* I shall be in until one fifteen, telephone me when he's gone.

GARRY. I'm lunching with him. He won't go. I can't give you a detailed report of his love life over the telephone with him in the room *(DOORBELL rings.)*

LIZ. *(Crossing to him)* Well, dial my number and when I answer just say, "I'm sorry—wrong number," then I shall know.

GARRY. What will you know?

LIZ. That everything's all right. But if you say I'm so *terribly* sorry it's a wrong number, I'll know that everything's all wrong and be round in a flash to back you up.

GARRY. Intrigue! My whole existence is enmeshed in intrigue.

LIZ. Have you got that clear? Sorry, it's a wrong number, everything alright, *so* terribly sorry, it's a wrong number, everything all wrong. *(Ad lib phone bus.)*

GARRY. Yes.

LIZ. Will you promise to do it?

GARRY. Yes! *(The DOORBELL rings again—crossing to Center)* I'll tell you another fascinating thing about my life here if you care to hear it. Nobody in this house ever answers a bell under a half an hour. *(He shouts)* Miss Erikson— Fred—

LIZ. I'm going now, remember I shall be in until I hear from you. *(DOORBELL rings.)*

GARRY. Miss Erikson!— Fred! Monica! (MISS ERIKSON *comes hurriedly out of the kitchen)* The front door bell, Miss Erikson, has been pealing incessantly for twenty minutes.

MISS ERIKSON. Alas yes, but there's a woman at the back door with a tiny baby.

GARRY. What does she want?

MISS ERIKSON. I do not know, there was no time to ask her. (MISS ERIKSON *goes out into the hall.)*

GARRY. Most of the silver's gone by now, I expect.
MONICA. *(Enters Left)* Did you call?
GARRY. Monica, there's a woman at the back door with a tiny baby! Go and deal with her.
MONICA. *(Crossing Up Center)* What does she want?
GARRY. *(With frigid patience)* That can only be discovered by asking her. Kindly do so.
MONICA. There's no need to snap at me. (MONICA *goes off through the kitchen.)*

(LIZ *puts on her hat and coat.* MISS ERIKSON *re-enters from front door.)*

MISS ERIKSON. *(Announcing)* Mr. Maule.

(ROLAND MAULE *enters. He is an earnest young man with glasses. He is obviously petrified with nerves but endeavoring to hide it by assuming an air of gruff defiance.* MISS ERIKSON *goes to kitchen.)*

GARRY. *(Advancing with great charm)* How do you do?
ROLAND. How do you do?
GARRY. This is my wife— Mr. Maule. She just popped in for a minute and is now about to pop out again.
ROLAND. Oh! How d'you do? Goodbye.
LIZ. *(Crossing to piano, picks up her umbrella)* Don't forget, Garry. I'll be sitting by the telephone.
GARRY. *(Ad lib—telephone business. Crosses to sofa)* I'll remember.

(LIZ *goes out front door.)*

GARRY. *(Motions* ROLAND *into a chair)* Do sit down, won't you?
ROLAND. *(Sitting chair Center)* Thank you.
GARRY. *(Crossing back of Center chair)* Cigarette?
ROLAND. No, thank you.
GARRY. Don't you smoke?

ROLAND. No.

GARRY. *(Crossing Down Center)* Drink?

ROLAND. No, thank you. *(Leg up.)*

GARRY. How old are you?

ROLAND. Twenty-five. Why?

GARRY. It doesn't really matter— I just wondered.

(Pause.)

ROLAND. How old are you?

GARRY. Forty in December— Jupiter you know—very energetic.

ROLAND. Yes, of course. *(He gives a nervous, braying laugh.)*

GARRY. *(Crosses and sits on sofa)* So—you've come all the way from Uckfield?

ROLAND. It isn't very far.

GARRY. Well, it sort of sounds far, doesn't it?

*(*MONICA *comes in from kitchen.* ROLAND *rises.)*

MONICA. *(Crossing to back of sofa)* It's a sweet little thing, but it looks far from well.

GARRY. What did she want?

MONICA. Her sister.

GARRY. Well, we haven't got *her,* have we?

MONICA. She lives two doors down in the Mews. It was all a mistake.

GARRY. This is my secretary, Miss Reed— Mr. Maule.

ROLAND. How do you do?

(They shake hands.)

MONICA. How do you do— I have your script in the office if you'd like to take it away with you.

ROLAND. Thank you very much.

GARRY. Quickly!

MONICA. Yes, dear. *(Crosses to Left and exits into office and shuts door.)*

GARRY. Sit down. I want to talk to you about your play.

ROLAND. *(Sits armchair Center, gloomily)* I expect you hated it.

GARRY. Well, to be candid, I thought it was a little uneven.

ROLAND. I thought you'd say that.

GARRY. I'm glad I'm running so true to form.

ROLAND. I mean it really isn't the sort of thing you would like, is it?

GARRY. In that case why on earth did you send it to me?

ROLAND. I just took a chance. I mean I know you only play rather trashy stuff as a rule, and I thought you just might like to have a shot at something *deeper.*

GARRY. What is there in your play that you consider so deep, Mr. Maule? Apart from the plot which is completely submerged after the first four pages.

ROLAND. Plots aren't important, it's ideas that matter. Look at Chekov.

GARRY. In addition to ideas I think we might concede Chekov a certain flimsy sense of psychology, don't you?

ROLAND. You mean my play isn't psychologically accurate?

GARRY. *(Gently)* It isn't very good, you know, really it isn't.

ROLAND. I think it's very good indeed.

GARRY. I understand that perfectly, but you must admit that my opinion might be the right one, based on a lifelong experience of the theatre.

ROLAND. *(Contemptuously)* The commercial theatre.

(Pause.)

GARRY. Oh dear, oh dear, oh dear.

ROLAND. I suppose you'll say that Shakespeare wrote for the commercial theatre and that the only point of doing anything with the drama at all is to make money!

All those old arguments. What you don't realize is that the theatre of the future is the theatre of ideas.

GARRY. That may be, but at the moment I am occupied with the theatre of the present.

ROLAND. *(Rises. Heatedly)* And what do you do with it? Every play you appear in is exactly the same, superficial, frivolous and without the slightest intellectual significance. You have a great following and a strong personality, and all you do is prostitute yourself every night of your life. All you do with your talent is to wear dressing-gowns and make witty remarks when you might be really helping people, making them think! Making them feel!

GARRY. There can be no two opinions about it. I am having a most discouraging morning.

ROLAND. *(Sits next to* GARRY*)* If you want to live in people's memories, to go down to posterity as an important man, you'd better do something about it quickly. There isn't a moment to be lost.

GARRY. I don't give a hoot about posterity. Why should I worry about what people think of me when I'm dead as a doornail anyway? My worst defect is that I am apt to worry too much about what people think of me when I'm alive. But I'm not going to do that any more. I'm changing my methods and you're my first experiment. *(Rise)* As a rule, when insufferable young beginners have the impertinence to criticize me, I dismiss the whole thing lightly because I'm embarrassed for them and consider it not quite fair game to puncture their inflated egos too sharply. But this time, my highbrow young friend, you're going to get it in the neck. To begin with your play is not a play at all. It's a meaningless jumble of adolescent, pseudo-intellectual poppycock. It bears no relation to the theatre or to life or to anything. *(Crosses to chair Center)* And you yourself wouldn't be here at all if I hadn't been bloody fool enough to pick up the telephone when my secretary wasn't looking. Now that you are here, however, I would like to tell you this. If you wish to be a playwright you just leave the theatre of tomorrow to take care of itself. Go and get yourself a job as a butler in a repertory company if they'll have you. Learn from the ground up how plays are constructed and what is actable and what isn't. Then sit down and write at least twenty plays one after the other, and if you can manage to get the twenty-first produced for a Sunday night performance you'll be God-damned lucky! *(Sits pouffe.)*

ROLAND. *(Rises. Hypnotized)* I'd no idea you were like this. You're wonderful!

GARRY. *(Flinging up his hands)* My God!

ROLAND. *(Crossing to him)* I'm awfully sorry if you think I was impertinent, but I'm awfully glad too because if I hadn't been you wouldn't have got angry, and if you hadn't got angry I shouldn't have known what you were really like.

GARRY. You don't in the least know what I'm really like.

ROLAND. Oh yes, I do—now.

GARRY. I can't see that it matters anyway.

ROLAND. It matters to me.

GARRY. Why?

ROLAND. Do you really want to know?

GARRY. What are you talking about?

ROLAND. It's rather difficult to explain really.

GARRY. What is diffcult to explain?

ROLAND. *(Bends down)* What I feel about you.

(Pause.)

GARRY. *(Rises; crossing to Center)* Now—look here, young man.

ROLAND. *(Crossing to Right of him)* No, please let me speak—you see in a way I've been rather unhappy about you—for quite a long time—you've been a sort of obsession with me. I saw you in your last play forty-seven times; one week I came every night, because I was up in town trying to pass an exam.

GARRY. Did you pass it?

ROLAND. No, I didn't.

GARRY. I'm not entirely surprised.

ROLAND. My father wants me to be a lawyer, that's what the exam was for, but actually I've been studying *psychology* a great deal because I felt somehow that I wasn't at peace with myself and gradually, bit by bit, I began to realize that *you* signified something to me.

GARRY. What sort of something?

ROLAND. I don't quite know—not yet.

GARRY. That "not yet" is one of the most sinister remarks I've ever heard. *(Crosses to door Left.)*

ROLAND. Don't laugh at me, please. I'm always sick if anyone laughs at me.

GARRY. You really are the most peculiar young man.

ROLAND. I'm all right now, though, I feel fine! *(Crosses to Left Center.)*

GARRY. I'm delighted.

ROLAND. *(Crosses to* GARRY*)* Can I come and see you again?

GARRY. I'm afraid I'm going to Africa.

ROLAND. Would you see me if I came to Africa too?

GARRY. Oh, no—no, I think you'd be much happier in Uckfield. *(Crosses back of sofa to Center.)*

ROLAND. I expect you think I'm mad, but I'm not really. I just mind deeply about certain things. But I feel much better now because I think I shall be able to sublimate you all right.

GARRY. Good! Now I'm afraid I shall have to turn you out because I'm expecting my manager and we have some business to discuss.

ROLAND. *(Crossing to Center)* It's all right. I'm going immediately.

GARRY. *(Crossing Left)* I'll get you your script.

ROLAND. No, no—tear it up—you were quite right about it—it was only written with part of myself. I see that now. Goodbye—goodbye.

GARRY. Goodbye.

ROLAND. Goodbye!

(ROLAND *goes out front door.* GARRY *runs to the office door.)*

GARRY. Monica.

MONICA. *(Entering Left, crossing to front of Center table)* Has he gone?

GARRY. *(Front of chair Center)* If ever that young man rings up again get rid of him at all costs. He's mad as a hatter.

MONICA. Why, what did he do?

GARRY. He started by insulting me and finished by sublimating me.

MONICA. Poor dear, you look quite shattered. Have a glass of sherry.

GARRY. *(Sits chair Center)* Those are the first kind words I've heard this morning.

MONICA. I think I'll have a nip too. *(She pours out two glasses of sherry.)*

(The front DOORBELL rings. MISS ERIKSON *runs on through the kitchen door to hall door.)*

GARRY. What time is it?

MONICA. Twenty to one. That's Morris. Here you are, dear— *(She gives him his sherry.)*

(There is the sound of voices outside. HUGO *and* MORRIS *come in, followed by* MONICA. HUGO *is rather dapper and neat. His age is about forty.* MORRIS *is a trifle younger, tall and good looking and a little grey at the temples.)*

HUGO. Hello, Monica.

MORRIS. Hello, Monica.

MONICA. Hello.

HUGO. *(Crossing back of sofa)* There's a strange young man sitting on the stairs.

GARRY. What's he doing?

HUGO. *(Crossing Down Right Center)* Crying.

MORRIS. What have you been up to, Garry?

(ERIKSON *enters hall and exits to kitchen.)*

GARRY. I haven't been up to anything. I merely told him what I thought of his play.

HUGO. I'm glad to see you haven't lost your touch.

MONICA. *(At bar)* Sherry, Morris?

MORRIS. Thanks.

MONICA. *(Gives him some)* Hugo?

(MORRIS *crosses to Right of pouffe.)*

HUGO. Is it the same sherry that you always have?

MONICA. Yes.

HUGO. No, thank you.

GARRY. Why, what's the matter with it?

HUGO. Nothing much, it's just not very nice. *(Crosses down Left. Lights cigarette.)*

GARRY. You ought never to have joined the Athenaeum Club, it's made you pompus.

MORRIS. Hugo's quite right about the sherry, it's disgusting.

(MONICA *sits pouffe.)*

GARRY. *(Rise)* If anybody complains about anything else I shall go raving mad. *(Crossing Left)* This studio's been like a wailing wall all the morning. *(Crossing Center.)*

MORRIS. What's the matter with the old boy, Monica? He seems remarkably crotchety.

MONICA. Liz was just here and she went for him a bit and then I told him he overacted, he really has had rather a beastly time and then that dotty young man on top of everything. (GARRY *crosses down front of Center table.)*

MORRIS. *(Crosses to* GARRY*)* Never mind, Garry—

God's in His heaven and all's right with the world—I've got some lovely bad news for you.

GARRY. I know. I wrote that.

MORRIS. We'll have to rehearse a new leading woman.

GARRY. Why?

MORRIS. Nora Fenvick can't come to Africa.

GARRY. Why?

MORRIS. She's broken her leg.

(Pause.)

GARRY. *(Sits sofa. Exasperated)* Well, really—!!

(Pause.)

HUGO. *(Sits)* It isn't actually so terribly important.

GARRY. Oh, not at all, it couldn't matter less! Weeks of rehearsal—six plays. (HUGO *sits down Left)* How did the silly bitch do it?

MORRIS. She fell down at Victoria station.

GARRY. She'd no right to be at Victoria station. *(To* HUGO) Who can we get?

HUGO. Well, Morris wants Beryl Willard but I don't think she's quite right.

GARRY. *(Dangerously)* So you want Beryl Willard, do you?

MORRIS. Why not? She's extremely competent.

GARRY. *(With intense quietness)* I agree with you. Beryl Willard is extremely competent. She has been extremely competent for well over forty years. In addition to her competence she has contrived, with uncanny skill, to sustain a spotless reputation for being the most paralyzing, epoch-making, monumental, world-shattering, God-awful bore that ever drew breath!

MORRIS. Now really, Garry, I don't see—

GARRY. *(Warming up)* You don't see? Very well, I will explain just one thing further, and it's this. No prayer, no bribe, no threat, no power, human or divine, would induce me to go to Africa with Beryl Willard. I wouldn't go across the street with Beryl Willard.

MONICA. *(Rises; crossing to bar)* What he's trying to say is he doesn't care for Beryl Willard.

MORRIS. All right, she's out. Whom do you suggest?

HUGO. *(Rise)* Just a minute, if you're going to start one of those casting arguments I'm going. (MORRIS *Breaks down Right)* I've got to catch a plane for Brussels.

GARRY. What are you going to Brussels for anyhow?

HUGO. *(Crossing back of sofa)* Business. Nice ordinary, straightforward business. I can't wait to get there. *(Takes Left shoulder)* Goodbye, Sweetie. *(Jabs Right shoulder.)*

GARRY. Don't pound people.

HUGO. Try to be a little more amiable when I come back.— Goodbye, Morris—by the way, you might call up Joanna, she's all alone.

MORRIS. I have. I'm taking her to the opening at the Haymarket tomorrow night.

HUGO. Fine—goodbye, Monica! *(Goes out the front door.)*

MONICA. *(Crosses towards the office)* Goodbye! Do you want me any more?

GARRY. Why, what are you going to do?

MONICA. I'm going to write to Beryl Willard and ask her to come and live with you. (MONICA *goes off Left.)*

(Pause.)

GARRY. So you're taking Joanna to the Haymarket tomorrow night are you?

MORRIS. Yes, why?

(Pause.)

GARRY. I think I shall come too.

MORRIS. *(Front of pouffe)* All right, that'll be grand. I've got a box, there's lots of room.

GARRY. Why have you been so mournful lately?

MORRIS. I haven't been in the least mournful.

GARRY. Oh yes, you have, Liz has noticed it and so have I.

MORRIS. Well, you're both quite wrong. I'm perfectly happy.

GARRY. *(Irritably, walking about the room)* You like Joanna, don't you?

MORRIS. Of course I do, she's a darling.

GARRY. I wouldn't call her a darling exactly, but then I don't see very much of her. I gather you do.

MORRIS. *(Crossing Right Center)* What are you getting at?

GARRY. People are talking, Morris.

MORRIS. *(With an edge on his voice)* What about?

GARRY. About you and Joanna.

MORRIS. Rubbish!

GARRY. It's perfectly true, and you know it.

MORRIS. I don't know anything of the sort.

GARRY. Are you in love with her?

MORRIS. In love with Joanna? Of course I'm not.

GARRY. Do you swear to me that you haven't had an affair with Joanna?

MORRIS. *(Puts glass on mantel)* I'm damned if I'll be cross-questioned like this.

GARRY. Have you or haven't you?

MORRIS. *(Crossing to Right of pouffe)* Mind your own business.

GARRY. *(Rises; crossing to him)* My God, if this isn't my business nothing is. If you're fooling about with Joanna and Hugo finds out, do you realize what it will mean?

MORRIS. I refuse to go on with this conversation.

GARRY. You can refuse until you're blue in the face, you're going to listen to me.

MORRIS. *(Crossing front of chair Center. Shaking him off)* Leave me alone. *(WARN Curtain.)*

GARRY. Sit down, Morris, this is serious.

MORRIS. *(Sits chair Center— GARRY follows)* I've no

intention of submitting to one of your famous finger wagging tirades— I'm sick to death of them.

GARRY. *(Center)* Very well, I'm not going to ask you one more question, I'm not even going to bellow at you, much, but that all depends upon whether or not you annoy me. I am however going to make you see one thing clearly, and it is this. You and Hugo and Monica and Liz and I share something of inestimable importance to all of us, and that something is mutual respect and trust. God knows it's been hard won. We can look back on years and years of bitter conflict with ourselves and with each other. But now, now that we're all middle-aged we can admit, with a certain mellow tranquility, that it's been well worth it. Here we are, five people closely woven together by affection and work and intimate knowledge of each other. It's too important a "setup" to risk breaking for any outside emotional reason whatsoever. *(Crossing back of sofa)* Joanna is alien to us. She doesn't really belong to us and never could. Hugo realizes that perfectly well, he's nobody's fool and to do him justice he has never tried to force her on us. But don't believe for a minute that Joanna isn't a potential danger, because she is! She's a hundred percent female, exceedingly attractive and ruthlessly implacable in the pursuit of anything she wants. If she could succeed in wreaking havoc among all of us I am quite certain she would leave no stone unturned. She's a scalp hunter, that baby, if I ever saw one, and all I implore you is this. *(Crosses to* MORRIS*—hand on shoulder)* Be careful! *(*MORRIS *starts to answer)* You need not even answer me but *Be Careful!* Is that clear? *(Crosses to Right Center.)*

(Pause.)

MORRIS. *(Rising. Crossing Up to bar)* Perfectly. I think I'll have a little more sherry. *(He helps himself.)*

GARRY. *(Crossing to phone table)* Calling the restaurant—never made a reservation.

MORRIS. There's no need, we can always go upstairs.

GARRY. Upstairs smells of potted shrimps, it won't take a minute to ring up. (MORRIS *drops Down Right of chair Center.* GARRY, *at telephone, with a radiant smile)* Hello— Oh, I'm sorry, it's a wrong number. *(He hangs up as he turns to* MORRIS *and laughs.)*

THE CURTAIN FALLS — MEDIUM FAST

ACT TWO

SCENE I

The time is midnight.. Three days have elapsed since Act I.

Night brackets on. Lamps and fire on. All doors closed. Move chair from hall to piano. Move bench into corner. Empty glass on piano.

GARRY *is playing the piano. When the Curtain rises the studio is pleasantly but not too brightly lit.* GARRY, *wearing a dressing-gown over his evening clothes. Presently* FRED *enters from the kitchen. He is very smartly dressed in a dinner jacket and he carries a soft black hat.*

FRED. *(Crossing Down foot of step)* Very pretty-very pretty indeed.

GARRY. You're very dressy! Where are you going?

FRED. Tagani's.

GARRY. Is it a dance hall or a night club or what?

FRED. Bit of all sorts really. Doris works there.

GARRY. What does she do?

FRED. Sings a couple of numbers and does a dance with a skipping rope.

GARRY. *(Rise)* Very enjoyable.

FRED. I think it's a bit wet if you ask me *(Turns away)* but still it goes down all right. *(Crosses down front of table.)*

GARRY. Are you going to marry Doris?

FRED. Me marry? What a hope!

GARRY. You know you really are dreadfully immoral, Fred.

FRED. *(Cheerfully)* That's right.

GARRY. *(Crossing to sofa Left; sits Left end)* I know

for a fact that you've been taking advantage of Doris for over two years now.

FRED. Why not? She likes it, I like it and a good time's 'ad by all.

GARRY. What will she do when we go to Africa?

FRED. She'll manage. She's got a couple of blokes running round after her now.

GARRY. Oh, I see, she's communal.

FRED. Will you ring in the morning as usual or do you want to be called? *(Crosses to Center.)*

GARRY. I'll ring. (FRED *starts)* Has Miss Erikson gone?

FRED. Oh yes, she went early. She 'ad a come-over about six o'clock and 'opped it. She's gone to 'er friend in Hammersmith. They turn out all the lights, play the gramophone and talk to an Indian.

GARRY. I suppose if it makes her happy it's all right.

FRED. She's a good worker even if she is a bit scatty and you can't 'ave everything, can you?

GARRY. No, Fred.

FRED. Will that be all? *(Crosses to platform.)*

GARRY. Yes, thank you, Fred. Enjoy yourself.

FRED. Same to you—be good. (FRED *goes out jauntily.)*

(GARRY *crosses to piano; gets glass; crosses to bar by front door. Presently the TELEPHONE rings.* GARRY *answers it.)*

GARRY. Allo, allo?— Who is that speaking? Please? *(His voice changes)* Oh, Liz— No, I've been in about half an hour— Yes, dear, quite alone, I'm turning over a new leaf—hadn't you heard? I went to the play with them last night, to supper at the Savoy afterwards and Morris and I dropped her home.— No, I didn't go on about it any more, I thought it wiser not. You sound a little skeptical— No, as a matter of fact she was very charming, she's quite intelligent you know and I must say she's a permanent pleasure to the eye— All right—

All right— I'm going straight to bed now alone— Good night, Liz darling.

(He hangs up. He goes Up Right to the drum table, gets book, switches off the LIGHTS and is half-way upstairs when the front DOORBELL rings. He mutters "Damn" softly, comes down and switches on the LIGHTS again and goes out into the hall and is heard to say "Joanna" in a surprised voice. She comes in and he follows her. JOANNA *is an exquisitely gowned woman in the early thirties. She has a great deal of of assurance and considerable charm.)*

JOANNA. *(Top of stairs)* I can't tell you how relieved I am that you're in. I've done the most idiotic thing.

GARRY. Why, what's happened?

JOANNA. I've forgotten my latchkey!

GARRY. Oh, Joanna!

JOANNA. *(Crossing to fireplace)* It's no good looking at me like that— I'm not in the least inefficient as a rule, this is the first time I've ever done such a thing in my life. I'm in an absolute fury. I had to dress in the most awful rush to dine with Freda and get to the Toscanini concert and I left it in my other bag.

GARRY. And I suppose the servants sleep at the top of the house?

JOANNA. They do more than sleep, they apparently go off into a coma. I've been battering on the door for nearly a half hour.

GARRY. Would you like a drink?

JOANNA. Very much indeed— I'm exhausted. *(She takes off her cloak.)*

(Pause.)

GARRY. *(Mixing a drink for her and himself at bar)* We must decide what's best to be done.

JOANNA. I went to a telephone booth just now and rang up Liz but she must be out because there wasn't any reply. *(Sits pouffe.)*

GARRY. *(Looking at her)* You rang up Liz and there wasn't any reply!

JOANNA. Yes, and I hadn't any more change and the taxi man hadn't either, I came straight here.

(GARRY *crosses to* JOANNA—*hands her drink.)*

GARRY. Here you are.

JOANNA. Thank you.

GARRY. Cigarettes?

JOANNA. No—thank you—you're looking very whimsical, don't you believe me?

GARRY. Of course I believe you, Joanna, why on earth shouldn't I?

JOANNA. I don't know, you always look at me as though you didn't trust me an inch. It's a shame because I'm so nice really.

GARRY. *(Smiling)* I'm sure you are, Joanna.

JOANNA. I know that voice, Garry, you used it in every play you've ever been in.

GARRY. *(Crosses and gets chair Right. Sits)* Complete naturalness on the stage is my strong suit.

JOANNA. *(Turn to him)* You've never liked me really, have you?

GARRY. No, not particularly.

JOANNA. I wonder why.

GARRY. I always had a feeling you were rather tiresome.

JOANNA. In what way tiresome?

GARRY. Oh, I don't know. There's a certain arrogance about you, a little too much self-assurance.

JOANNA. You don't care for competition, I see.

GARRY. You're lovely-looking, of course, I've always thought that.

JOANNA. *(Smiling)* Thank you.

GARRY. If perhaps a little too aware of it.

JOANNA. *(Turn Down Center)* You're being conventionally odious but somehow it doesn't quite ring true. But then you never do quite ring true, do you? I expect it's because you're an actor, they are always apt to be a bit papier mache.

GARRY. Just puppets, Joanna dear, creatures of tinsel and sawdust, how clever of you to have noticed it.

JOANNA. I wish you'd stop being suave, just for a minute.

GARRY. What would you like me to do, fly into a tantrum? Burst into tears?

JOANNA. *(Looking down)* I think I should like you to be kind.

GARRY. Kind?

JOANNA. Yes. At least kind enough to make an effort to overcome your perfectly obvious prejudice against me

GARRY. I'm sorry it's so obvious.

JOANNA. I'm not quite an idiot, although I must say you always treat me as if I were. I know you resented me marrying Hugo, you all did and I entirely see why you should have, anyhow at first. But after all that's five years ago, and during that time I've done my best not to obtrude myself, not to encroach on any special preserves. My reward has been rather meagre, from you particularly, nothing but artficial politeness and slightly frigid tolerance.

(Pause.)

GARRY. Poor Joanna.

JOANNA. *(Rises; crossing Up Center)* I see my appeal has fallen on stony ground. I'm so sorry.

GARRY. What is all this? What are you up to?

JOANNA *(Puts glass down on table Up Right)* I'm not *up* to anything.

GARRY. Then sit down again.

JOANNA. I'd like you to call me a taxi.

GARRY. *(Crossing to* JOANNA*)* Nonsense, there's

nothing you'd hate more. You came here for a purpose, didn't you?

JOANNA. Of course I did. I lost my key, I knew you had a spare room and—

GARRY. Well?

JOANNA. *(Turn to him)* I wanted to get to know you a little better.

GARRY. I see.

JOANNA. *(Crossing toward back of sofa)* Oh no, you don't. I know exactly what you think. Of course I can't altogether blame you. In your position as one of the world's most famous romantic comedians, it's only natural that you should imagine that every woman is anxious to hurl herself at your head. I'm sure, for instance, that you don't believe for a moment that I've lost my latchkey!

GARRY. You're good— My God, you're good!

JOANNA. *(Cross to phone)* What's the number of the taxi rank— I'll ring up myself.

GARRY. *(Crossing back of sofa)* Sloane 2664.

(Pause.)

JOANNA *(Dials the number and waits a moment)* Hallo—hallo— Is that Sloane 2664?— Oh! it's the wrong number. Oh! The line's engaged! What are you laughing at?

GARRY. You, Joanna.

JOANNA. *(Dialing again)* You're enjoying yourself enormously, aren't you?

GARRY. *(Taking the telephone out of her hand)* You win.

JOANNA. Give me that telephone and don't be so infuriating.

GARRY. Have another drink?

JOANNA. No, thank you.

GARRY. A cigarette?

JOANNA. No.

GARRY. Please— I'm sorry.

JOANNA. *(Takes a cigarette)* I wish you *were* really sorry.

GARRY. *(Lights* JOANNA'S *cigarette)* Maybe I am.

(Pause.)

JOANNA. I could cry now, you know very effectively, if only I had the technique.

GARRY. Technique's terribly important.

JOANNA. Oh dear. *(Crosses to Right end of sofa; sits.)*

(Pause.)

GARRY. *(Crossing back of sofa to* JOANNA) Conversation seems to have come to a standstill.

JOANNA. I think perhaps I would like another drink after all, a very small one.

GARRY. *(Crosses to bar)* Good. Soupcon.

JOANNA. You make me feel extraordinarily self-conscious. Of course that's one of your most renowned gifts, isn't it—frightening people?

GARRY. *(Pouring out a drink)* You're not going to pretend that I frighten you.

JOANNA. It's personality, I expect, plus a reputation for being—well— *(She laughs)* rather ruthless.

GARRY. *(Crossing to* JOANNA) Amorously or socially?

JOANNA. Both. *(Takes drink from* GARRY*—sips it.)*

(Pause.)

GARRY. *(Crossing to Center)* Well— How are we doing?

JOANNA. Better I think.

GARRY. That's a very pretty dress.

JOANNA. I wore it for Toscanini.

GARRY. *(Sits chair Center)* He frightens people too, when they play the wrong notes.

JOANNA. *(Puts glass down)* You look strangely

young every now and then. It would be nice to know what you were really like, under all the trappings.

GARRY. Just a simple boy, stinking with idealism.

JOANNA. Sentimental too, almost Victorian at moments.

GARRY. I spend hours at my sampler.

JOANNA. Are you happy on the whole?

GARRY. Ecstatically.

JOANNA. You never get tired of fixing people's lives, of being the Boss, of everybody adoring you and obeying you?

GARRY. Never. I revel in it.

JOANNA. I suspected that you did but I wasn't sure.

(Pause.)

GARRY. Would you like me to play you something?

JOANNA. No, thank you.

GARRY. Why ever not? You must be mad!

JOANNA. Not mad, just musical.

GARRY. Snappy too. Quite rude in fact.

JOANNA. Yes, that was rather rude, wasn't it? I'm sorry.

(Pause.)

GARRY. Never mind. What shall we *do* now?

JOANNA. Do? Is there any necessity to do anything?

GARRY. I don't know, my social sense tells me that something is demanded of me and I'm not quite sure what it is. That's why I suggested playing to you.

JOANNA. I'm so glad I'm adult. You must be pretty shattering to the young and inexperienced. You glitter so brightly.— All the little bells tinkling.

GARRY. *(Crosses to side of chair Center)* I sound like a circus horse.

JOANNA. You are rather like a circus horse as a matter of fact! Prancing into the ring to be admired, jumping, with such assurance, through all the paper hoops.

GARRY. Now listen, Joanna. You've got to make up your mind. This provocative skirmishing is getting me down. What do you want?

JOANNA. I want you to be what I believe you really are, friendly and genuine, someone to be trusted. I want you to do me the honor of stopping your eternal performance for a little, ring down the curtain, take off your makup and relax.

GARRY. Everyone keeps telling me to relax.

JOANNA. One can hardly blame them.

GARRY. Shouldn't I be very vulnerable, dear Delilah, shorn of my nice silky hair?

JOANNA. Why are you so afraid of being vulnerable? I should think it would be rather a relief? To be perpetually on guard must be terribly tiring.

GARRY. I was right about you from the first.

JOANNA. Were you?

GARRY. You're as predatory as hell!

JOANNA. Garry!

GARRY. *(By Right end of sofa)* You got the wretched Hugo when he was convalescent, you've made a dead set at Morris, and now by God you're after me! Don't deny it— I can see it in your eye. You suddenly appear out of the night reeking with the lust of conquest, the whole atmosphere's quivering with it! You had your hair done this afternoon didn't you? And your nails and probably your feet too! That's a new dress, isn't it? Those are new shoes! You've never worn those stockings before in your life! And your mind, even more expertly groomed to vanquish than your body. *(Crosses to Right Center)* You want to know what I'm really like, do you under all the glittering veneer? Well, this is it.— Fundamentally honest! When I'm driven into a corner I tell the truth, and the truth at the moment is that I know you, Joanna, I know what you're after, I can see through every trick. *(Move in)* Go away from me! Leave me alone!

JOANNA. *(Laughing)* Curtain!

GARRY. *(Crossing Up to bar)* Damn it, there isn't any more soda-water.

JOANNA. Take it neat, darling.

GARRY. How dare you call me darling.

JOANNA. Because I think you are a darling— I always have. You're really the reason I married Hugo.

GARRY. *(Crossing Down back of chair Center)* Are there no depths to which you won't descend?

JOANNA. Absolutely none. I'm in love with you— I've been in love with you for over seven years now, it's high time something was done about it.

GARRY. *(Crossing Right. Striding about)* This is the end!

JOANNA. *(Rises; crosses front Left end of sofa. Calmly)* No, my sweet, only the beginning.

GARRY. Now listen to me, Joanna—

JOANNA. I think you better listen to me first.

GARRY. *(Crossing Up Center)* I shall do no such thing.

JOANNA. *(Calmly and with great firmness)* You must, it's terribly important to all of us. Please sit down. *(Indicating Right end of sofa.)*

GARRY. *(Crossing back of sofa to Down Left then crossing Right)* I'd rather walk about if you don't mind.

JOANNA. Sit down, dear sweet Garry, please sit down. I've got to explain and I can't if you're whirling about all the time.

GARRY. *(Crossing and flinging himself onto sofa, Right end)* This is dreadful!

JOANNA. First of all I want you to promise me to answer one question absolutely truthfully. Will you?

GARRY. What is it? *(WARN Curtain.)*

JOANNA. If you had never seen me in your life before, if we had met for the first time tonight, if I were in no way concerned with anyone you know, would you have made love to me. Would you have wanted me? *(Pause.)*

GARRY. Yes.

JOANNA. Well, that's that. *(Sits)* Now then—

GARRY. Look here, Joanna—

JOANNA. Shut up! You must be fair, you must let me explain. When I said just now that you were the reason I married Hugo, that was only partly true. I'm devoted to Hugo, much fonder of him really than he is of me. Hugo has been lightly unfaithful to me eleven times to my certain knowledge during the last three years. He's probably having a high old time in Brussels at this very moment.

GARRY. You're lying Joanna.

JOANNA. I'm not lying. I don't *mind* enough to lie. Hugo's a darling and I wouldn't leave him for anything in the world, but you're the one I'm in love with and always have been.

GARRY. *(Bitterly)* What about Morris? Is he in love with you? Has there been anything between you?

JOANNA. Of course there hasn't.

GARRY. Do you swear to that?

JOANNA. There's no need for me to swear it, you can see can't you? I don't want to live with you, God forbid. You'd drive me mad in a week. But you are to me the most charming, infuriating, passionately attractive man I've ever known. *(Leans over him. Touching his arm)* Who could you and I possibly harm by loving each other for a while? *(Pause.)*

GARRY. Please may I get up now? (JOANNA *removes her hand. Shakes her head and kisses him. The LIGHTS fade and:*

THE CURTAIN FALLS— FAST

ACT TWO

SCENE II

The time is about ten thirty the next morning. The curtains are drawn and the studio is dim.

JOANNA *comes out of the bedroom Right wearing pyjamas and the same dressing-gown that* DAPHNE *wore in Act I She wanders around the room for a bit looking for a bell.* MISS ERIKSON *comes out of kitchen.*

JOANNA. *(Front of mirror, brightly)* Good morning.

MISS ERIKSON. Good morning.

JOANNA. *(Stops Right Center)* Is Mr. Essendine awake yet?

MISS ERIKSON. He has not rung. *(She goes over and draws the curtains.)*

JOANNA. I wonder if you'd be very kind and tell him that *I* am awake.

MISS ERIKSON. *(Crosses to table Left)* Alas, no. He would be crazy with anger.

JOANNA. Would he indeed! I shall be crazy with anger myself unless I have some breakfast. I have been ringing that bell in there for hours.

MISS ERIKSON. *(Crosses to fireplace)* It does not work.

JOANNA. Oddly enough that dawned on me after a while.

MISS ERIKSON. It is the mice, they eat right through the wires, they are very destructive.

(FRED *comes out of kitchen, whistling, he goes up on landing.)*

JOANNA. Good morning.

FRED. *(At top of steps)* Good morning, Miss— *(He recognizes her)* Oh dear!

JOANNA. *(Crosses back of sofa)* I beg your pardon?

FRED. You're Mrs. Lyppiatt, aren't you?

JOANNA. Yes, I am.

FRED. *(Whistling)* Whew! *(He goes off again through the kitchen door.)*

JOANNA. *(Crossing back of table Center)* That I gather was Mr. Essendine's valet. Does he always behave like that?

MISS ERIKSON. *(Crossing to Right Center)* He was a steward on a very large ship.

JOANNA. Most of the ship's stewards I've met have good manners.

MISS ERIKSON. *(Crossing to Center)* He is the only one I know.

JOANNA. *(Peremptorily)* Would you bring me some china tea, some thin toast without butter and a soft-boiled egg, please.

MISS ERIKSON. We have no tea and no eggs either, but I will make the toast with pleasure. *(Crosses up on platform.)*

JOANNA. Is there any coffee?

MISS ERIKSON. Yes, we have coffee.

JOANNA. Well, please bring me some as quickly as you can.

MISS ERIKSON. *(Move up Center)* I will tell Fred.

JOANNA. And as he was on such a large ship, perhaps he could do something about the faucet in that bathroom.

MISS ERIKSON. Alas, he was not a bathroom steward. (MISS ERIKSON *goes off to kitchen.)*

(Just as JOANNA *with an exclamation of irritation, crosses back of Left end of sofa,* MONICA *comes in from the hall in a hat and coat. As in Act I, she carries a bundle of letters.)*

MONICA. Joanna?

JOANNA. Good morning, Monica.

MONICA. *(Horrified crosses to top of steps)* Joanna!

JOANNA. Thank heaven you've come, I've had such a complicated chat with the housekeeper.

MONICA. *(Crosses back of Center table)* Did you stay the night here?

JOANNA. Yes, wasn't it sweet of Garry to let me? I did the most idiotic thing. I lost my latchkey.

MONICA. You lost your latchkey?

JOANNA. I was in absolute despair and then I suddenly thought of Garry.

MONICA. You suddenly thought of Garry!

JOANNA. Why do you keep repeating everything I say?

MONICA. *(Crosses down Center)* I don't know, it seems easier than saying anything else.

JOANNA. Why, Monica, you actually look as if you disapproved of my staying the night here!

MONICA. I think it was tactless to say the least of it.

JOANNA. *(Crosses Left to front of phone table)* In heaven's name why? It was a perfectly natural thing to do in the circumstances.

MONICA. When is Hugo coming home?

JOANNA. Tomorrow morning on the eleven o'clock plane. Is there anything else you'd like to know? *(Sit sofa Left, takes off slippers; legs on sofa).*

MONICA. No, I don't think I want to know anything else at all.

JOANNA. I must say, Monica, I really do resent your manner a litle bit, anyone would think I'd done something awful.

MONICA. Obviously you are a better judge of that than I.

JOANNA. It's quite astounding to think that anyone as close to Garry as you have been for so many years should have a lewd mind.

MONICA. I'm sure you must be shocked to the marrow.

JOANNA. *(With great poise)* I really don't feel equal to continuing this rather strained conversation before I've had some coffee. Perhaps you'd be kind enough to hurry it up for me.

MONICA. I always knew it. *(Starts up.)*

JOANNA. *(Irritably)* Always knew what?

MONICA. That you'd cause trouble. I'll see about your coffee. *(The front DOORBELL rings)* There's somebody at the door, you'd better go back into the spare room.

JOANNA. I'm quite happy here, thank you.

MONICA. As you please. *(She goes to the front door.)*

(After a moment's pause she comes in again followed by LIZ. LIZ *to whom the news has only just been broken, is wearing a set expression. She is however quite calm.)*

LIZ. Good morning, Joanna.

JOANNA. *(Turns around)* Liz!

LIZ. This *is* a surprise.

JOANNA. I tried to get you for hours last night. I'd lost my latchkey and was in the most awful state. But you weren't in.

LIZ. *(Crossing Down Center)* I was in from ten o'clock onwards. You must have been ringing the wrong number.

JOANNA. I rang the number you gave me.

LIZ. *(Sweetly)* Then I must have given you the wrong number.

MONICA. *(Crosses back of sofa to Down Left)* If you want me, Liz, I shall be in the office.

LIZ. I do want you, Monica, so don't budge.

(FRED *comes in with a tray.)*

JOANNA. *(With rather overdone relief)* Ah, breakfast.

FRED. *(Crosses back of sofa to table Left)* Where will you 'ave it?

JOANNA. Here, please.

(FRED *stops back of sofa.)*

LIZ. I think it would be more comfortable for Mrs. Lyppiatt to have her coffee in the spare room.

JOANNA. *(Firmly)* I'd rather have it here, if you don't mind. I like to see what's going on.

LIZ. Put it down there for a moment, Fred, we will decide later where Mrs. Lyppiatt is going to have her coffee.

(FRED *puts tray on phone table, then crosses to back of Center table.)*

JOANNA. I've already decided, Liz, but it's sweet of you to take so much trouble.

LIZ. That will be all, thank you, Fred.

FRED. Rightyo, Miss— Give us a shout if you want anything.

LIZ. Thanks— I will.

(FRED *vanishes through the kitchen door. Pause.)*

JOANNA. *(Pouring out her coffee)* I understand he used to be a steward on a liner.

LIZ. *(Moves to back of chair Center. To* MONICA) I suppose Garry hasn't been called yet, has he?

MONICA. No, I don't think so. Shall I go and wake him now?

LIZ. No, not yet.

JOANNA. He really should be wakened at once, Liz. It's disgraceful lying in bed on a lovely morning like this—so unhealthy. He'll be getting fat and flabby if he's not careful.

MONICA. *(In heartfelt tones)* I wish to God he would.

JOANNA. I wonder what she put in this coffee, apart from the coffee, I mean.

MONICA. Weed killer if she had any sense.

JOANNA. You're really being remarkably offensive, Monica. One always hears that the secretaries of famous men are rather frustrated and dragon-like.

MONICA. The only thing that's frustrating me at the

moment is a wholesome fear of the gallows. (MONICA *goes into the office and slams the door.)*

JOANNA. *(Takes coffee)* Poor thing, she's aged a lot since I first met her. I suppose she's mad about Garry like all of us? *(Puts coffee cup down.)*

LIZ. *(Crossing Down Center; sits chair Center)* All of *us*, Joanna?

JOANNA. I must say he is enchanting. We had the most lovely talk last night.

LIZ. I think it would be better if neither Hugo or Morris knew you stayed the night here, Joanna.

JOANNA. Good heavens, why? Hugo wouldn't mind a bit.

LIZ. I wouldn't be too sure if I were you, anyhow Morris would.

JOANNA. Morris? What on earth has Morris to do with it?

LIZ. *(Rising. With irritation)* Now listen, we haven't much time to waste fencing with each other. I know perfectly well that you have been unfaithful to Hugo with Morris, so you needn't trouble to deny it any further.

JOANNA. It's the most abominable lie—

LIZ. *(Crossing to sofa)* Unfortunately I dined quietly with Morris last night, at the Ivy. He was very upset and became rather hysterical, as you know he sometimes does, and he told me everything. *(Sits on sofa.)*

JOANNA. How dare he discuss me with you, or with anybody.

LIZ. I don't think Garry would like to know that you had been Morris's mistress as well as Hugo's wife. I don't think Morris would like to know that you have been Garry's mistress, which I suspect you have.

JOANNA. What are you talking about?

LIZ. And I don't think Hugo would like to know anything about any of it.

JOANNA. Are you trying to blackmail me?

LIZ. Yes, I am.

JOANNA. You mean that you'd be low enough to tell Garry?

LIZ. Yes. And Morris and Hugo. I'll tell them all unless you do as I say.

JOANNA. I suppose you're still in love with Garry yourself.

LIZ. I certainly do love him. I love Hugo and Morris too. We've all been devoted to one another for many years. And I'm not taking any risks of you even upsetting it temporarily. You're going to do what I tell you.

(Pause.)

JOANNA. And what if I don't? *(Rise.)*

LIZ. You'll be out, my dear, with all of us, forever. With Garry most of all—quite soon.

JOANNA. *(Turn to* LIZ*)* You're very sure.

LIZ. Absolutely positive. I know Garry very well, you know. After all, I've had every opportunity.

JOANNA. *(Crossing to Center)* It's a pity you ever left him.

LIZ. For him yes, I think it is.

JOANNA. And *why* should you imagine that I should mind—so terribly—being "out" with all of you as you put it?

LIZ. Because you made such a terriffic effort to get in. You'd have had better results and much quicker too, if you hadn't been so determined to be alluring.

JOANNA. *(Crossing to pouffe; sits)* I've never been talked to like this in my life.

LIZ. *(Rises; crosses to* JOANNA*)* Are you going to be sensible and do what I ask you or not?

JOANNA. You haven't asked me anything yet.

LIZ. I want you to promise me that you won't see Garry again before he goes to Africa.

JOANNA. Well really!

LIZ. Will you promise that?

JOANNA. No, certainly not. It's nonsense. I'm bound to see him again. How can I avoid it?

LIZ. You can be ill. You can go to Paris. Anywhere.

JOANNA. I have no intention of doing any such thing.

LIZ. Very well. *(Crossing bottom of steps Up Center)* Fred—Fred.

JOANNA. It will be you who's breaking everything up, not me.

FRED. *(Enters from kitchen)* Did you call, Miss?

LIZ. *(Back of table)* Go and wake Mr. Garry immediately, will you?

FRED. Rightyo— *(He starts to go when the front DOORBELL rings.)*

LIZ. You'd better answer the door first. *(To* JOANNA. *Crossing back of sofa)* It's Morris.

JOANNA. *(Rise)* Morris! How do you know?

LIZ. He told me last night he was coming to see Garry at eleven.

JOANNA. *(Rises. Crossing to* LIZ *as* FRED *goes to front door)* Look here, Liz—

LIZ. I'm glad really, it'll be more convenient.

JOANNA. *(Turn away Right hurriedly)* I can't face him. It'll be too unpleasant. I'll do what you say.

LIZ. *(Follows* JOANNA*)* You swear it? You swear you won't see him again? You'll go away?

JOANNA. Yes, yes— I swear it.

LIZ. Quickly, go back to the spare room. And don't come out until I tell you..

(JOANNA *darts into the room Right and shuts the door.)*

FRED. *(Comes back)* It's Mr. Maule. He says he has an appointment.

LIZ. Mr. what?

FRED. Maule. He looks a bit wet to me.

LIZ. Oh, dear—well, I suppose you'd better show him in— Miss Reed can deal with him— I'll tell her.

FRED. Rightyo.

(FRED *goes back to the front door.* LIZ *flies over to the office door.)*

LIZ. *(In an urgent whisper)* Monica—Monica—
MONICA. *(Appearing)* Yes—what is it?
LIZ. *(Back of sofa)* A Mr. Maule is here.
MONICA. *(Crossing to table Left)* He's no right to be, he's raving mad.
FRED. *(Announcing)* Mr. Maule.

(ROLAND MAULE *enters.)*

ROLAND. *(Nervously. Top of steps)* How do you do? We met before, do you remember?
LIZ. Yes, very well—just the other day.
MONICA. *(Crossing to front of sofa)* Have you an appointment with Mr. Essendine?

(LIZ *crosses back of pouffe.)*

ROLAND. *(Crossing to* MONICA. *Obviously lying)* Oh yes, indeed. I spoke to him on the telephone last night. He told me I was to come at ten-thirty. I fear I'm a little late.
MONICA. I'm afraid you can't see him at the moment. Could you come back later?
ROLAND. Isn't there anywhere I could wait?
MONICA. *(Pushes him to door Left)* Go into the office for a moment and I'll find out when Mr. Essendine can see you.
ROLAND. It's very kind of you—thanks very much. *(As* MONICA *puts him into the office and shuts the door)* Thank you.
FRED. Oughtn't I to have let 'im in?
MONICA. I don't know. He says Mr. Garry told him to come although I can hardly believe he did. You'd better go and wake him and ask him.
LIZ. No, Monica. Don't wake Garry yet. I'd rather he slept on a bit.

MONICA. All right, Fred. We'll call him later.

FRED. It's all the same to me. (FRED *goes off to the kitchen.)*

(MONICA *crosses to* LIZ *Right of sofa.)*

LIZ. Listen, Monica. I've guaranteed that you and I won't say a word to Hugo or Morris or anybody about her being here if she swears not to see Garry again before he goes.

MONICA. Did she?

LIZ. Yes, she did. But Morris will be here at any moment and it's going to be awkward. There's a telephone in the spare room, isn't there?

MONICA. Yes.

LIZ. Is it the same number as this or different?

MONICA. It's the private wire. This one is an extension of the office.

LIZ. What's the number?

MONICA. You know it—the private line— Sloane 2642.

(The front DOORBELL rings.)

LIZ. There he is, leave this to me. I'll explain later. *(She rushes over to bedroom Right and goes in, closing the door behind her.)*

(FRED *comes in and goes to the front door.)*

MONICA. *(Goes to the office and opens the door)* Oh, Mr. Maule, what are you doing? *(She goes in and shuts the door.)*

(GARRY *appears at the top of the stairs, fully dressed, with a hat on. He creeps downstairs and meets* MORRIS, *who has entered front door, face to face.)*

MORRIS. Garry! Where are you going?

GARRY. *(A little flustered)* Out.

MORRIS. Out where? (MORRIS *crosses Down Right Center.)*

GARRY. I suppose I can go out if I want to, can't I?

FRED. I never even knew you was up! You are a dark 'orse and no mistake.

GARRY. Don't be impertinent, Fred, and go away.

FRED. *(Crossing to Right of* GARRY) All right—all right. The gentleman's in the office and the lady's in the spare room if you 'appen to want either of 'em. (FRED *goes off cheerfully to kitchen.)*

MORRIS. Lady! What lady?

GARRY. What's he talking about! The boy's off his rocker.

MORRIS. Really, Garry, you're impossible. Who's in there?

GARRY. I would be very much obliged if everybody would mind their own God-damned business.

MORRIS. For heaven's sake get rid of her— I've got to talk to you— I'm in a bad way—

GARRY. What's the matter?

MORRIS. Get rid of *her* first, whoever she is.

GARRY. How can I get rid of her, she may be in the bath.

MORRIS. Tell her to hurry then.

GARRY. Now look here, Morris—

MORRIS. *(Crossing to Right)* If you won't— I will. *(He strides over Right to the bedroom door.)*

GARRY. *(Crossing Down Center)* Morris— I forbid you to go near that room.

MORRIS. *(Loudly knocking on the door)* Will you please come out—as soon as you can. *(Crosses back Right Center.)*

(LIZ *enters Right closing the door behind her.)*

MORRIS. Liz! It's you!

GARRY. It's you!

LIZ. Of course. Who did you think it was?

GARRY. Yes. Who'd you think it was?
MORRIS. What on earth were you making such a fuss about Garry?
GARRY. I make a fuss? I don't know what you mean!
LIZ. *(Crossing to* GARRY*)* Why are you so completely dressed so very suddenly? You were asleep a few minutes ago!

(MORRIS *moves Down Right.)*

GARRY. Oh no I wasn't. I most gravely doubt whether I shall ever be able to sleep again.
LIZ. Perhaps your conscience was troubling you.
GARRY. *(Crossing front of sofa)* I cannot for the life of me imagine why everybody is so absolutely beastly to me! *(Sits sofa, Left)* To be away from the lot of you.
LIZ. It won't be exactly unrelieved sadness for us.
GARRY. No sarcasm, please.
MORRIS. *(Crossing to Center)* For God's sake stop bickering, both of you. I'm in the most awful state.
GARRY. What about?
MORRIS. Liz knows— I told her last night.
GARRY. What does Liz know? What did you tell her last night?
LIZ. *(Whispers)* Pull yourself together, Morris. Have a drink or something. Try not to be silly.
MORRIS. *(Whispers)* I don't want a drink. If I have a drink it will make it much worse. It always does.
GARRY. This is a most fascinating little conversation, but I must say I should appreciate the full flavour of it more if I had just an inkling as to what it was all about.
MORRIS. *(Crossing to Center)* I haven't slept for three nights, Garry—ever since you talked to me the other morning.
GARRY. Why not?

(LIZ *backs a step Left.)*

MORRIS. It's bad enough getting one of my awful obsessions. You know what I'm like when I get an obsession. God knows you've helped me through enough of them, but this time I've made an utter fool of myself and *(Sits chair Center)* lied to you into the bargain.

GARRY. *(Sharply)* Lied to me? What do you mean?

MORRIS. *(Drops his head)* Joanna and I love each other.

GARRY. *(After a slight pause—looking at* LIZ) Oh!

LIZ. Oh, dear.

MORRIS. It's been going on for several months, but we made a pact that we'd lie about it to everyone, whatever happened, in order not to make an awful mess and upset everything. But I'm not used to lying to you—and it's been driving me mad. Yesterday afternoon I couldn't bear it any longer and I told Joanna I was going to tell you. She was furious and said she'd never speak to me again if I did and went away and left me. I've been trying to find her ever since. She's disappeared. Her servants say she hasn't been home all night. I'm so terrified that something has happened to her.

LIZ. Perhaps it has.

MORRIS. You don't like her, Liz you never did. I'm not sure that I do really, but I love her.

(Pause.)

LIZ. It's all very fragrant, isn't it, Garry? *(Crosses to Left of sofa. Pause)* You needn't fuss any more, Morris. Joanna spent the night with me.

MORRIS. Spent the night with you!

LIZ. *(Viciously)* Yes, on the sofa. She lost her latchkey. (GARRY *rises, crosses Right)* She's there now. I told her I'd tell you to ring her up if I saw you. *(Crosses to phone.)*

MORRIS. *(Rise)* I'll go around now.

LIZ. *(Dialing)* No. You'd better ring up first—and see if she's still there—she may have gone out. I'm getting the number for you. *(She dials a number.* GARRY *watches her fascinated)* Hallo—Maggie? Is Mrs. Lyppiatt still there?— All right— Here you are, Morris— *(She hands him the telephone and comes over to* GARRY.)

MORRIS. *(Rise, crosses to phone and picks it up)* Joanna!— Yes, it's me, Morris.

LIZ. *(Quietly to* GARRY) You unutterable fool!

MORRIS. I've been terribly worried, why didn't you tell me you were with Liz—

GARRY. *(Hissing to* LIZ) How did you get her out?

LIZ. She's not out, she's in there, on the other line.

(Pause.)

MORRIS. —I thought something had happened to you. —Yes, I'm at the studio—No, only Liz and Garry— Yes, I have, I had to—How can you be so cruel!— Listen, Joanna— I must see you—Joanna!— *(To* LIZ *and* GARRY) She's hung up!

GARRY. Serves you right.

MORRIS. *(Crossing to* GARRY) I must see her— I must see her—what am I to do?

GARRY. Control yourself and don't be hysterical.

MORRIS. *(Crossing up to step)* I'm going to Liz's flat now.

LIZ. No!

GARRY. *(Crossing Up Left)* No. You're not. You're coming with me.

MORRIS. Coming with you? Where to?

GARRY *(At random)* Westminster Abbey.

MORRIS. *(Crossing Up to* GARRY) It's cruel and heartless of you to try to be funny at a moment like this.

(Ad lib fight.)

GARRY. I'm not trying to be funny at all. What's the matter with Westminster Abbey. It's historic! (MONICA *enters Left)* What do you want? *(Pours out a drink at bar for* MORRIS *and hands it to him.)*

MONICA. Did you or did you not give an appointment to Mr. Maule this morning?

GARRY. *(Crossing to front of sofa)* I most emphatically did not. He terrifies the life out of me.

MONICA. Well, he's here—

ROLAND. *(Comes out of the office)* I'm afraid I told a wicked lie about the appointment but I must see you—it's very, very important.

MONICA. Please, Mr. Maule.

ROLAND. *(Crossing to* GARRY. *Ignoring her)* I want to tell you that it's all right.

GARRY. What's all right?

(MORRIS *crosses back of sofa.)*

ROLAND. *(Eagerly)* About what I felt about you—I've got the whole thing straightened out.

GARRY. I'm absolutely delighted and I congratulate you from the bottom of my heart, but you really must go away now.

(There is a ring at the front DOORBELL.)

MONICA. Please go now, Mr. Maule. Mr. Essendine is in the middle of a conference.

GARRY. Like hell I am! *(Crosses up Center. The DOORBELL rings again, insistently)* —Miss Erikson! —(ERIKSON *enters from kitchen)* There's somebody at the door. I have not the remotest idea who it is but I strongly suspect that it is a silly son of a bitch who is madly in love with me!

(ROLAND *crosses and sits chair Center.* ERIKSON *goes to door.)*

LIZ. Mr. Maule, I really do think it would be better if you were to come back later.

ROLAND. Couldn't I stay a little longer? You see every

moment I'm near him I get smoother and smoother and smoother, my whole rhythm improves tremendously.

HUGO. *(Comes in from front door He is obviously in a state of great agitation. On steps)* Where's Joanna? She's disappeared.

(ERIKSON *going into kitchen.)*

GARRY. I thought you weren't coming back until to-morrow.

HUGO. She hasn't been home all night, nobody knows where she is.

LIZ. It's all right, Hugo, she stayed with me.

HUGO. *(Crosses Down Center)* But I rang up Maggie and she said she hadn't seen her.

LIZ. *(Crossing to* HUGO) There's a reason for that, I'll explain later. *(Crosses down Right.)*

HUGO. *(Down Center)* Something's happened. I had a presentiment in the aeroplane.

GARRY. I always have a presentiment in an aeroplane, a presentiment that I'm going to be sick! I think I'm going to be sick up here.

HUGO. But why did Maggie say—

LIZ. Ring her up if you don't believe me. Monica, get my flat on the telephone—

(MONICA *goes to the telephone and proceeds to dial the number.)*

ROLAND. *(Going to* HUGO *and shaking hands with him)* How do you do, my name is Roland Maule.

HUGO. *(Abstractedly)* How do you do?

ROLAND. *(Crossing to* MORRIS. *Shaking hands with* MORRIS) Roland Maule, I don't think we've met.

GARRY. *(Hypnotic gesture)* Back to your nest, Mr. Maule.

(ROLAND *sits on chair Right of piano.)*

MONICA. *(At telephone)* Hallo—Joanna?— Hold on a minute, Hugo wants to speak to you— Yes, he's here —in the studio— *(She hands the telephone to* HUGO.)

(MONICA *sits chair Left.)*

HUGO. *(Crosses in front of sofa to phone)* —Darling —you gave me the most awful fright— No, I got through everything yesterday and there was no sense in staying— I sent a telegram— No, I couldn't think what had happened— Yes, we're all here— Are you coming back to the house?— All right, I'll be in to change in about half an hour— Very well, darling— I'll tell her— *(To* LIZ) She says she's going out in a minute.

GARRY. Oh!

LIZ. Tell her to stay where she is, I'll pop in and see her presently.

(DOORBELL. FRED *enters from kitchen and answers door.)*

HUGO. *(At telephone)* Liz says to stay where you are and she'll be round presently— What!—

GARRY. What's she say?

HUGO. *(To* LIZ) She says she feels as if she were in a French farce. She sounds upset.

LIZ. *(Crossing in a step)* That's the telephone, it never stops ringing. Tell her to shut it off. *(Breaks Right.)*

HUGO. *(At telephone)* Liz says you're to shut off the telephone— Joanna— Hallo— *(To* EVERYONE*)* She's hung up. *(During the preceding conversation the front DOORBELL has rung again.* FRED *now returns.)*

FRED. There's a Lady Saltburn outside.

GARRY. Lady who?

FRED. Lady Saltburn, she says she has an appointment for eleven thirty.

MONICA. *(Rising)* Good heavens! What's today?

GARRY. *(Crossing Down Center)* Black Thursday.

MONICA. *(Crossing to* GARRY) Thursday— I'd completely forgotten— Lady Saltburn's niece—you promised you'd give her an audition and recommend her to the Royal Academy or something, don't you remember?

GARRY. No, I do not. She must be sent away immediately.

MONICA. We can't send Lady Saltburn away, she gave us fifty pounds for the Footlights Fund.

GARRY. How can I possibly listen to people's nieces this morning? I'm on the verge of a nervous breakdown already. *(Crosses to Right Center.)*

HUGO. Why, what's happened?

GARRY. *(Sits pouffe)* Too much, Hugo! Far, far too much!

MONICA. You must see her.

GARRY. No.

MONICA. It won't take a minute.

GARRY. No.

MONICA. It would be most terribly rude not to, after all you promised.

GARRY. No.

MONICA. Ask her in, Fred.

FRED. Rightyo. *(He goes to the front door.)*

(Ad lib.)

MORRIS. *(Crossing to Right of* ROLAND) We'd better go— I'll come back later, Garry— Liz, Hugo—

HUGO. *(Crossing front of sofa to* MORRIS) All right. We'll go to Liz's flat and talk to Joanna.

MORRIS. *(In a panic)* No— I must go to the office and you must come with me—it's urgent.

ROLAND. *(Rise. With his braying laugh)* It's all very exciting, isn't it?

FRED. *(Announcing)* Lady Saltburn. Miss Stillington! *(Exits to kitchen.)*

GARRY. *(Bitterly)* Thank you, Monica, you're a great comfort to me!

(LADY SALTBURN *enters, accompanied by* DAPHNE STILLINGTON. LADY SALTBURN *is a majestic but rather effusive society woman.* DAPHNE *is wearing a set expression of social poise. There is a glint in her eye.)*

LADY SALTBURN. *(Crosses to* GARRY *Right)* Mr. Essendine, this is so charming of you.

GARRY *(Shaking hands)* Not at all—it's a pleasure.

LADY SALTBURN. This is my niece, Daphne. I believe you knew her mother years ago, she died, you know—in Africa.

GARRY. *(Crossing to* DAPHNE) How shocking!

DAPHNE. I've been longing to meet you, Mr. Essendine. *(With intensity)* I've loved everything you've ever done.

GARRY. *(Shakes hands with* DAPHNE) How very nice of you.

LADY SALTBURN. Daphne simply wouldn't give me peace until I had rung up your secretary and absolutely implored her for an appointment. She's so tremendously keen, you know—

GARRY. She must be. *(He shoots* DAPHNE *a look of fury)* I must introduce you to everybody. My wife. My secretary. Miss Reed—

LADY SALTBURN. *(Crossing to* MONICA) How do you do, you were so kind on the telephone.

GARRY. Mr. Dixon— Mr. Lyppiatt—and Mr. Mole—Mule— Maule!

(MONICA *sits Down Left.)*

LADY SALTBURN. *(Crosses and sits pouffe)* Oh, this is quite a peep behind the scenes. *(Turn away Right.)*

GARRY. One peep is quite enough.

DAPHNE. *(Crossing to* GARRY) This is the most thrilling moment of my life, Mr. Essendine, I've always wondered what you'd be like close to.

LADY SALTBURN. You mustn't embarrass Mr. Essendine, Daphne.

DAPHNE. I'm sure he understands—don't you, Mr. Essendine?

GARRY. Of course, my dear, I understand perfectly, but I'm afraid I can only give you just a few minutes—you see I'm terribly busy just now making arrangements for my tour— *(He shoots a look at* LADY SALTURN*)* in Africa.

LADY SALTBURN. I'd no idea you were going to Africa, how very interesting. You really must pay a visit to my brother-in-law, he lives on the most beautiful mountain—on the top.

GARRY. *(Crossing to* LIZ*)* God— I can hardly wait.

HUGO. *(Crossing to* LADY SALTBURN*)* I do hope you'll forgive us but we have to go now.— Goodbye.

LADY SALTBURN. How sad—goodbye.

HUGO. Liz?

LIZ. I'm staying here for a little— I'll come later.

MORRIS. *(Crossing to her)* Goodbye, Lady Saltburn— *(He bows to* DAPHNE*)* Goodbye.

(DAPHNE *breaks Right Center.)*

GARRY. Goodbye, Mr. Maule.

ROLAND. I'm staying too.

(HUGO *and* MORRIS *go out front door.* MONICA *and* LIZ *exchange glances of relief.* DAPHNE *takes a step to* GARRY; GARRY *crosses Left back of sofa to Down Left.)*

LADY SALTURN. Are you ready, Daphne? You know how busy Mr. Essendine is— I'm sure it's very sweet of him to see us at all— We mustn't impose on him.

(GARRY *front of sofa to Center.)*

DAPHNE. *(Crossing to* LADY SALTBURN. *Almost defiantly)* Yes— I'm ready.

GARRY. *(Crossing to* DAPHNE) What are you going to do?

DAPHNE. *(Looking into his eyes)* Nothing very much— I'll try not to bore you. You see I want you to hear me so very much—it means everything to me—you will hear me, won't you—you can hear me, can't you?

LADY SALTBURN. Daphne—really! What are you talking about?

DAPHNE. Mr. Essendine understands, don't you, Mr. Essendine?

GARRY. Mr. Essendine understands everything. He spends his whole life understanding absolutely everything and what nobody else seems to understand is that the strain of it is driving him step by step to a suicide's grave! *(Sits chair Center.)*

LIZ. Don't be affected, Garry.

GARRY. My wife, Lady Saltburn, left me several years ago. Gnawing regret has embittered her.

ROLAND. There's nothing worse than regret. Look at Chekov! He knew.

GARRY. We have no time at the moment to look at Chekov, Mr. Maule. *(To* DAPHNE) What are you going to do, *sing?* Please don't be nervous.

DAPHNE. I'm not nervous, but I wish you weren't so many miles away. I'm not going to sing— I'm just going to say a few lines—

GARRY. Charming—fire away.

DAPHNE. *(Stands Left of pouffe and looks at him fixedly. She begins)*

"We meet not as we parted—

GARRY. Shelley!

DAPHNE.

"We feel more than all may see;
My bosom is heavy-hearted
And thine full of doubt for me
One moment has bound the free."

GARRY. Nothing that Shelley didn't know.

DAPHNE.

"That moment has gone forever— *(Stop.)*

GARRY. *(Prompting her)*
Like lightning—
DAPHNE.
"Like—lightning that flashed and died
Like a snowflake upon the river
Like a sunbeam upon the tide— *(Stops.)*
GARRY. *(Rises. Prompting)*
That moment—

(During the last verse, JOANNA *comes swiftly out of the spare room. She is wearing her evening dress and cloak of the night before. She is obviously extremely angry.)*

JOANNA. *(Furiously. Crossing to* GARRY) That room is like a frigidaire and I have no intention of staying in it one minute longer. Will somebody kindly call me a taxi?

DAPHNE. *(Breaking off. Turns to* LADY SALTBURN) Oh!— Oh, dear!

LIZ. You'd better take my car, Joanna, it's downstairs.

DAPHNE. *(One step towards* JOANNA. *Violently)* The chauffeur's got red hair and his name's Frobisher!

LADY SALTBURN. *(Pulling* DAPHNE *by skirt)* Daphne!

JOANNA. Thank you very much. *(To* GARRY) I shan't see you again, Garry, as I am going to Paris tomorrow for a month so this is goodbye. I do hope that when you go to Africa you will be wise enough to take all your staunch, loyal satellites with you. It's too dangerous for a little tinsel star to go twinkling off alone and unprotected. Please don't imagine that I haven't enjoyed the circus enormously. Because I have. *(Crosses up on platform)* But in the circuses I've been used to it was always the ringmaster who cracked the whip, not the clown. Goodbye! *(She sweeps out front door.)*

(DAPHNE *gives a loud cry and faints dead away.* LADY SALTBURN *and* MONICA *run to her.)*

ROLAND. *(Jumps on piano. Exultantly)* This is splendid! Splendid! I feel reborn!

GARRY. *(Runs upstairs)* Oh, go to hell!

FAST CURTAIN

ACT THREE

A week has passed since the preceding Act.

The time is between nine and ten in the evening GARRY *is leaving for Africa first thing in the morning, so there are various trunks and suitcases about. There has been a farewell cocktail party, so there is a buffet table with remains on it and the whole place is dotted with glasses and ashtrays. Coffee table set in front of sofa. Wastebasket by chair Center.*

GARRY, *with the inevitable dressing gown over his suit is enjoying a light meal at a coffee table.* MONICA *is seated on the chair Center with a large tray of letters on her lap, around her on the sofa are scattered several more.*

When the Curtain rises, MONICA *is reading a letter aloud.*

MONICA. *(Sitting chair Center)* "—I shall never forget those lovely days in Madeira and our picnics on the rocks, what fun we had. It really was wonderful getting to know you intimately. Now for my exciting news. I am coming to England. Imagine! I arrive on the twenty-eighth and shall be in London for three whole weeks. You remember you told me to let you know a good time beforehand if I should be coming so I am doing so. I am so longing to see you again. With my love and many glorious memories. Yours, Winnie."

GARRY. When's it dated?

MONICA. November the seventh.

GARRY. Over six months ago. She must be gone by now. Much too late to answer it.

MONICA. Much.

GARRY. Poor Winnie.

MONICA. *(Tearing it up)* She'd probably have been an awful nuisance anyhow. Don't forget your ship stops at Madeira in a few days' time. You'd better lock yourself in your cabin.

GARRY. Not at all. If I run into her I shall say I never got the letter and that it's my secretary's fault.

MONICA. It's your fault. These letters have been stacking up for months. Here's one signed "Joe."

GARRY. Joe what?

MONICA. Just "Joe." It's dated March the second.

GARRY. Let's look.

MONICA *(Handing it to him)* He seems to have met you in the south of France.

GARRY. I do get about, don't I? *(Looking at the letter)* Oh, it's Joe.

MONICA. *(Patiently)* That's what I said.

GARRY. Joe was marvelous. I met him in a bar in Marseilles. He's dark green and comes from Madras. *(Pause)* What does he want?

MONICA. It's at the end, after the bit about his sister having a baby.

GARRY. Oh, yes—well, why didn't you send him one?

MONICA. Because I didn't consider that "Joe, Madras" was sufficient address.

GARRY. I'm damned if I can remember his last name.

MONICA. *(Taking it from him and tearing it up)* Well, *He's* out of luck then, isn't he?

GARRY. I wonder if I shall ever see my green England again.

MONICA. I see no reason why you shouldn't.

GARRY. I might die of some awful tropical disease or be bitten by a snake.

MONICA. I doubt if there *are many* snakes in the *larger* cities.

GARRY. I can see myself now under a mosquito net, fighting for breath—

MONICA. Who with?

GARRY. Dear, dear Monica, you have no imagination. Just a flat literal mind. It must be very depressing for you.

MONICA. I get by.

GARRY. How many more are there to do?

MONICA. About twenty.

GARRY. I can't bear it. Put them away until I come back.

MONICA. You seemed to be in doubt just now as to whether you *were* coming back.

GARRY. Well, I can't answer letters if I'm dead, can I? Not a moment's peace ever in my life—not even a tranquil hour when I can say farewell to my books and pictures— I slave and slave—and what do I get?

MONICA. *(Rises; crossing to fire)* Nonsense, you've got the whole evening to say farewell to your books and pictures.

FRED. *(Comes in from the kitchen and crosses Down Center. He's in evening dress again. Picks up tray from coffee table and starts)* 'Ave you finished with the tray? I want to be getting along.

GARRY. What can I say? Is everything packed?

FRED. *(Up Center)* All except the last minute stuff, we can pop that in in the morning.

GARRY. Is this poor Doris's swan song?

FRED. 'Ow d'you mean?

GARRY. Nothing, Fred—it couldn't matter less.

(FRED *disappears in kitchen with the tray.)*

MONICA. *(Gathering up the letters)* I must be going home.

GARRY. Don't leave me alone— I feel depressed.

MONICA. *(Crossing to table Left)* You were screaming for peace just now. I'll be here first thing in the morning.

GARRY. I wish you were coming with me. I shall be utterly lost with some dreary temporary African.

MONICA. Is Liz coming to the station?

GARRY. No.

MONICA. Why don't you go round and see her?

GARRY. You know perfectly well. She's still in a rage. I haven't seen her for a week.

MONICA. Have you tried?

GARRY. Of course I have. I've telephoned her three times. Each time she spoke to me kindly and remotely as if I were an idiot child. I'm not sure she didn't spell some of the words out to me.

MONICA. Would you like me to have a go at her?

GARRY. No. If she wants to behave like an outraged governess with chilblains she can get on with it.

MONICA. I see her point, you know. You really did go a little too far.

GARRY. Now, Monica, don't you start on me too.

MONICA. *(With a slight smile)* All right, I'll take these into the office. *(She goes into the office with the letters.)*

FRED. *(Comes out of the kitchen with his hat)* Nothing more you want?

GARRY. No, Fred.

FRED. It was quite a party, wasn't it? 'Ow many did we 'ave?

GARRY. I don't know, about sixty, I should think.

FRED. Sixty. Well, between 'em all they put away enough gin to float the *"Queen Mary."*

GARRY. You'd better call me at eight in the morning. We have to leave the house at ten.

FRED. *(Starts)* Rightyo.

GARRY. Good night, Fred—enjoy yourself.

FRED. Same to you—be good. *(Goes out front door.)*

(GARRY *walks about the room.)*

MONICA. *(Comes out of the office in her hat and coat)* Oh—by the way, you'd better be careful if the telephone rings. Roland Maule has been calling up all week.

GARRY. I think I'd almost welcome him tonight. At least he'd be interesting psychologically.

MONICA. So would Rasputin.

GARRY. *(Rises; crosses Up Center)* I feel dreadfully flat. I suppose one always does before going away.

MONICA. *(Crossing back of sofa to* GARRY*)* Now now now, you're getting a big boy, you know.

GARRY. Forty-two, my next birthday.

MONICA. Forty-one, isn't it? Good night, dear. See you in the morning. *(Crosses up Center.)*

GARRY. *(Crossing to Left of her)* I do envy you, Monica, you're so unruffled and efficient. You go churning through life like some frightening old warship.

MONICA. Thank you, dear, that sounds most attractive. Good night.

GARRY. Good night. Your propeller's showing. *(*MONICA *goes off. The TELEPHONE rings.* GARRY *flies to it. Jumps on trunk)* Hallo hallo— No, it isn't. *(He hangs up.)*

MISS ERIKSON. *(Comes out of the kitchen in her hat and coat)* I am going away now, Mr. Essendine. Have you everything you want? *(Crosses down Center.)*

GARRY. Frankly, Miss Erikson, no. I have nothing that I want.

MISS ERIKSON. Oh, what a pity.

GARRY. Have you? Have any of us—got what we want?

MISS ERIKSON. *(Back of chair Center. With a little laugh)* Oh, Mr. Essendine, you are only acting! For a moment you made me quite upset.

GARRY. *(Sits Left end of sofa)* You lead a strange life, Miss Erikson, do you enjoy it?

MISS ERIKSON. Yes, indeed.

GARRY. Tell me about it from A to Z.

MISS ERIKSON. Do you mind if I pinch a cigarette?

GARRY. Pinch anything you like, Miss Erikson.

(As MISS ERIKSON *moves toward cigarettes on table Center,* GARRY *jumps.)*

MISS ERIKSON. *(Taking several)* I smoke so much and I am always running out. It is most silly.

GARRY. Where are you going now, for instance?

MISS ERIKSON. I am going to my friend in Hammersmith. She is a German.

GARRY. Is she a spy?

MISS ERIKSON. Yes, I think so but she is very kind.

GARRY. I understand from Fred that she is a medium as well?

MISS ERIKSON. Oh dear, yes. Sometimes she makes a trance and it is very surprising. She will lie on the ground for many hours making noises.

GARRY. What kind of noises?

MISS ERIKSON. They are different. Sometimes she will sing high up like a bird and at other times she may make a little bark. Often she is very ill.

GARRY. I'm not at all surprised.

MISS ERIKSON. *(Takes cigarettes. Crossing Up to exit)* Well, I must be pushing off now.

GARRY. Thank you very much, Miss Erikson, it's been most interesting.

MISS ERIKSON. Not at all— Good night.

GARRY. Good night.

(MISS ERIKSON *goes out front door.* GARRY *takes off robe and puts coat on. Jumps slightly as DOOR-BELL rings, then goes to open it. In the hall his voice is heard saying "Daphne."* DAPHNE *comes in carrying a small dressing case. She is wearing a traveling coat and hat. She is rather nervous, but obviously determined.* BOTH *come to top of step.)*

GARRY. Daphne! What does this mean?

DAPHNE. I'm coming with you to Africa. I bought my ticket this afternoon—

GARRY. To Africa! !

DAPHNE. I've run away— I left a note for my aunt— you see I know something now— I've known it all the week really ever since that awful morning when I fainted — I know that you need me as much as I need you—

GARRY. Now, my dear child, really.

DAPHNE. No, please don't say anything for a moment — I've thought it all over very carefully. I know I'm very much younger than you and all that, but I can help you and look after you— *(Crosses to chair Center.)*

GARRY. Daphne dear, this is really too absurd. You must go home at once.

DAPHNE. *(Taking off her coat and putting it on chair Center)* I knew you'd say that. *(Crosses to back of sofa Left end.)*

GARRY. *(Crossing Down to* DAPHNE*)* Please put your coat on again and don't be silly.

DAPHNE. *(Crossing to front of sofa)* I felt ashamed on Thursday at first, ashamed at playing a trick on you by making Auntie ring up for an audition, but when I was here I was glad—

GARRY. Oh, so you were glad, were you?

DAPHNE. *(Exultantly)* Yes, I was. I think that's why I fainted. You see I suddenly realized the truth.

GARRY. *(Center)* What truth?

DAPHNE. How desperately lonely you really are, in spite of all those people round you, in spite of all your success— I knew how deep your longing must be to have someone really to love you, to be with you, and when I saw that dreadful prostitute come out of the spare room in that tawdry evening dress.

GARRY. That was not a prostitute. It was the wife of one of my dearest friends!

DAPHNE. No, Garry—you can't deceive me— I know.

GARRY. Once and for all, Daphne, I order you to put on your coat, get into a taxi and go straight back to your aunt.

DAPHNE. *(Crossing to* GARRY*)* No—you needn't be frightened— I won't make any demands on you whatever. I don't want you to marry me or anything like that. I don't believe that real love should be bound by Church or Law. Anyway I'm just coming with you, that's all. I'll just be there when you want me, when you're tired and lonely and want someone to put their arms round you. I won't even see you on the boat if you don't want me to. I'm not a very good sailor anyhow.

(The front DOORBELL rings.)

GARRY. That's the front door bell.

DAPHNE. Who is it?

GARRY. How do I know? You'd better go into the spare room.

DAPHNE. No, Garry, please not the spare room.

GARRY. That's what it's for.

DAPHNE. *(Crosses to door Right)* Get rid of them soon, promise, whoever it is.

GARRY. *(Crossing to* DAPHNE*)* Here's your coat—don't argue. *(He shoves her into the bedroom Right and goes to the front door.)*

(The following dialogue is heard off stage.)

GARRY. Mr. Maule.

ROLAND. *(Off)* Forgive me— I must see you.

GARRY. *(Off)* I'm very sorry you can't— I'm just going to bed.

ROLAND. *(Crossing to Right of trunk)* I'm afraid I must insist. You see it's a matter of life and death.

GARRY. Please come back at once. (ROLAND *comes in Down Center followed by* GARRY. GARRY *crosses Down to* ROLAND) What the hell do you mean by forcing yourself into my house like this?

ROLAND. That's right—shout—shout—you're magnificent when you're angry!

GARRY. *(Front of sofa)* I'll tell you something, young man—you're just raving bloody mad, that's all that's the matter with you.

ROLAND. Oh no, I'm not. You're the one who's mad.

GARRY. Will you please leave this house immediately.

ROLAND. I'm afraid I told a wicked lie just now when I said it was a matter of life and death.

GARRY. *(Crossing back of sofa to phone)* If you're not out of this house by the time I've counted ten I shall telephone for the police. 1-2-3-4-5-6-7-8-9-

ROLAND. I shan't let you. I'm tremendously strong, you know. I can lift the heaviest things imaginable without turning a hair.

GARRY. *(Changing his manner)* Now look here, Mr. Maule.

ROLAND. *(Sits sofa)* You may call me Roland.

GARRY. Thank you. Well, Roland, I want to put this situation to you reasonably and quietly. This is my last night in England and I have a great deal to do—

ROLAND. You said just now that you were going to bed.

GARRY. Be that as it may—

ROLAND. *(Interrupting)* I know you think I'm mad and I really don't blame you a bit, but I asure you I'm not at all. I merely have an exceptional brain, a brain that can be of inestimable service to you. As I told you the other day you signify a great deal to me.

GARRY. *(Crossing to Left Center)* I remember— I remember distinctly. I'm sure I'm very flattered, Roland.

ROLAND. *(Crossing to* GARRY*)* I—wonder if I could have a cookie?

GARRY. By all means, help yourself, Roland.

ROLAND. Thank you. I promise you faithfully I'll go after I've finished this cookie. After all there's no valid reason, is there, why I shouldn't be acting being mad just as you're acting being sane?

GARRY. I'm not acting.

ROLAND. You are always acting. That's what is so fascinating and you are so used to it that you don't even know it yourself. I am always acting too. I have been acting mad with you because it amuses me to see you put on a surprised face. I am absolutely devoted to your face in every mood. *(Crosses to him.)*

GARRY. I suppose you wouldn't like to act getting the hell out of here, would you?

ROLAND. *(Laughing wildly)* That's wonderful!

GARRY. Listen, what exactly do you want?

ROLAND. *(Sits chair Center)* To be with you. That's why I'm coming to Africa.

GARRY. That's why you're what! ! !

ROLAND. I bought a ticket today, it's steerage, but it's better than nothing. I have given up my law studies and left Uckfield for good. That's why I'm rather excitable tonight. You needn't be frightened that I shall get in your way or make any demands on you.

GARRY. You mean you don't expect me to marry you! I'll get you out of here. *(There is a ring at the DOOR-BELL)* There's somebody at the door. Do be a good boy, and go away now, will you? You promised you would when you finished your cookie.

ROLAND. I'm not going to allow you to turn me away. You'll regret it your whole life long if you do. I have a profound conviction about it that nothing will shake—

(ROLAND *suddenly rushes into the office, slams the door and turns the key in the lock.* GARRY *bangs helplessly on the door. The front DOORBELL rings insistently.)*

GARRY. Come out of that room immediately! Mr. Maule—Roland— Come out at once— Oh, my God!— *(Looks in mirror; takes a drink from bottle at bar. He goes out into the hall to open the front door.)*

JOANNA. *(After a moment* JOANNA *enters. She puts down bag on trunk Up Center)* Hallo, darling.

GARRY. What is the meaning of this, Joanna?

JOANNA. Don't you know?

GARRY. *(Top of steps)* Yes, I do. You're coming to Africa with me. You bought your ticket this afternoon. You're not going to make any demands on me and you're not a good sailor.

JOANNA. I'm a perfect sailor. What are you going to do about it? *(Crosses a step Center.)*

(GARRY *goes to the telephone. He dials a number. (Pause.)*

JOANNA. *(Puts purse on trunk)* What are you doing?

GARRY. *(With lips)* Telephoning. *(At telephone)* Hallo—hallo— Oh, I'm so terribly terribly terribly sorry, it's a wrong number! *(He hangs up.)*

JOANNA. *(Puts wrap on Center chair)* Who are you calling?

GARRY. *(With a grim smile)* It doesn't matter now. *(Puts receiver down. Crosses Down Left.)*

JOANNA. Darling. Underneath this rather taut, strained manner of yours, deep down inside, aren't you just a little bit glad to see me?

GARRY. *(Crosses to sofa and sits)* Absolutely delighted. It will settle things once and for all.

JOANNA. That's what *I* thought.

GARRY. When did you get back from Paris?

JOANNA. *(Crosses and sits sofa)* This afternoon. Did you get my telegram?

GARRY. Yes, Monica read it out to me.

JOANNA. I meant her to.

GARRY. I understood that you were going to stay in Paris for a month.

JOANNA. *(Shoes off)* No, you didn't, darling, you knew perfectly well I wouldn't. I must say I tried for the first few days, to put you out of my mind. I railed against you, said the most dreadful things that you weren't there to hear, then I remembered—

GARRY. What did you remember?

JOANNA. *(Legs up)* I remembered what you said to me the other night. You said "It doesn't matter what comes after this, what circumstances combine against us, what tears are shed! This is magic, the loveliest magic that I've ever known!"

GARRY. That's out of the second act of my play, "Love Is So Simple."

JOANNA. *(Feet on lap. Smiling)* Yes— I recognized it. I saw the play several times, you know.

GARRY. In that case why did you believe it?

JOANNA. I didn't. But the fact of your saying it proved something to me. It proved that you were no more sincere emotionally than I am, that you no longer *need* or *desire* the pangs of love, but are perfectly willing to settle for the fun of love. I couldn't agree with you more.

GARRY. *(Rises and crosses Down Left)* That, to date, is the most immoral statement I've ever heard in my life.

JOANNA. It's true though, isn't it?

GARRY. It's women like you who undermine the whole integrity of civilization!

JOANNA. What's that *out* of?

GARRY. The third act—it's not *out* of anything.

JOANNA. As I told you the other night, I've always wanted you. You're the first man I've ever met who's worthy of my steel. I can't guarantee that we shall be domestically happy together, but we'll have a good time.

GARRY. Joanna, please!

JOANNA. You were quite right when you said just now, with remarkable clairvoyance, that I was coming to Africa with you. I am I've got the bridal suite—

GARRY. The what! ?

JOANNA. —it was all there was left. In addition to that I've written a note to Hugo telling him everything.

GARRY. Everything.

JOANNA. He's dining with Morris. They can read it together. *(There is a ring at the DOORBELL)* Who's that? *(Legs down.)*

GARRY. With any luck it's the Censor.

(GARRY *runs out to front door.* LIZ *comes quickly in, followed by* GARRY. *She betrays no surprise upon seeing* JOANNA.)

GARRY. Oh, Liz. Terribly sorry, wrong number.

LIZ. *(Crossing Down Center)* Hullo, Joanna! (GARRY *to Right of* LIZ.)

JOANNA. *(Front of sofa)* Good evening, Liz dear, how nice you look.

LIZ. Thank you so much. I do my best.

JOANNA. I think it only fair to tell you. I'm sailing with Garry tomorrow.

LIZ. What fun, so am I.

GARRY. What!

LIZ. I decided this afternoon.

GARRY. *(Crossing Down Center)* What a day for that steamship company!

JOANNA. *(Perfectly controlled, but obviously angry)* If I may say so, Liz, I think that's rather silly of you.

LIZ. *(Up Center; puts things on trunk)* I really don't see why. It'll be charming. We can all eat at the same table and do our lifeboat drill together.

GARRY. Joanna has written a note to Hugo and Morris explaining everything.

LIZ. Good, then they'll probably be coming too.

GARRY. I should like to take this opportunity to say that I wish I were dead. *(Sits pouffe.)*

LIZ. Nonsense, darling, you'll enjoy the voyage enormously. There won't be a dull moment.

JOANNA. You imagine you're being very clever, Liz, don't you?

LIZ. I've learnt in a hard school.

JOANNA. Personally I think you're making the greatest mistake in your life. It's always foolish not to have the courage to admit defeat. *(Sits sofa.)*

LIZ. *(Crossing to back of table Right end of sofa)* You seem to imagine that I'm competing with you. I assure you I'm doing nothing of the sort. It's very important for all of us that this African tour of Garry's should be a success. Obviously there is no way of preventing you coming if you want to, but you'd better realize before it's too late that from the social and publicity angle you will be there as a friend of mine.

(There is a ring at the front DOORBELL.)

GARRY. I give you just three guesses as to who that is!

JOANNA. The gathering of the clans.

LIZ. I'll go, Garry. (LIZ *goes quickly to front door.)*

JOANNA. *(Takes jacket and purse from chair. Crossing to* GARRY. *Viciously)* Perhaps I've been wrong about you after all. You haven't got the guts of a rabbit!

GARRY. I'm very glad I haven't, I'm sure they'd be extremely inadequate.

(JOANNA *crosses to fireplace.* HUGO *and* MORRIS *come in,* LIZ *follows behind them.* BOTH *of them are palpably in a fury.)*

HUGO. *(To top of step)* Is it true? That's all I want to know. Is it true?

MORRIS. *(Crossing to* GARRY, *Right Center. Just a trifle intoxicated)* False friend! False friend!

(LIZ. *crosses back of sofa to Down Left.)*

GARRY. Come, come, Morris, you're not in the Athenaeum now.

HUGO. *(Crossing Down back of chair Center)* It's no good trying to be flippant. This is a miserable disgusting situation and you know it.

MORRIS. A stab in the back, that's what it is, a low down stab in the back.

GARRY. Not too low down, I hope.

LIZ. Shut up, Garry.

HUGO. I've had a note from Joanna. I suppose you know that, don't you?

JOANNA. Yes, he does. I've just told him.

HUGO. Is what she says in it true?

GARRY. How do I know? I haven't read it.

HUGO. Don't prevaricate. She says that you've been lovers and that you're going away together tomorrow. Is that true?

JOANNA. Perfectly true.

HUGO. *(Ignoring her)* Answer me, Garry. Answer me. *(Jumping up and down.)*

GARRY. *(Dangerously)* I'll tell you what's true and what's not true all right, and you can stop bouncing up and down like a rubber ball and listen—

LIZ. *(Warningly. Crossing front of sofa)* Be careful, Garry.

GARRY. *(Rises; crossing to Right of* MORRIS) Careful! I've been a damn sight too careful with the lot of you for years!

HUGO. Have you or have you not been Joanna's lover?

(LIZ *sits Down Left.)*

GARRY. Yes, I have.

MORRIS. You miserable cad!

GARRY. *(Crossing to* JOANNA) You came here the other night absolutely determined to get me, didn't you? And you were plausible and superficially alluring enough to succeed. You certainly roused my curiosity very cleverly. (JOANNA *turns away)* but it takes more than cleverness to touch my heart or my mind.

MORRIS. *(Violently)* You haven't got a heart or a mind. You haven't got one decent instinct in you. You're morally unstable and false through and through!

GARRY. *(Full out)* For the love of God, stop being theatrical! !

(MORRIS *crosses Up Right.)*

LIZ. Oh, dear.

GARRY. You should never have married Joanna in the first place, Hugo, I always told you it was a grave mistake.

HUGO. *(Crossing to* GARRY. *Furiously)* You have the damned impertinence to stand there after seducing my wife and—

GARRY. *(Sits* HUGO *Down on arm of chair Center)* Look here, Hugo, it's high time we got down to brass tacks. I didn't seduce your wife and well you know it. You're taking up a very high and mighty attitude over the whole thing, but I'm perfectly convinced that if you face the facts honestly for a minute you'll discover that you don't really mind in the least. Morris is the one who minds. For the moment.

HUGO. *(Rise)* Morris!

LIZ. Oh, Garry, that was disgraceful of you.

GARRY. *(Crossing Up Center)* Disgracful my foot! I'm fed up of everybody lying and intriguing and acting all over the place.

JOANNA. All right, Garry, you win. I wouldn't have believed anyone in the world could sink so low.

GARRY. *(Crossing down Center)* Fiddlesticks! *(Turns Up.)*

HUGO. *(Rise)* What did you mean about Morris? Answer me!

GARRY. *(Turn back)* I mean that Morris and Joanna have been carrying on an abortive little dingdong under your silly nose for months.

MORRIS. *(Crosses to* GARRY*)* I'll never speak to you again until the day I die!

GARRY. Well, we can have a nice chat then, can't we?

HUGO. *(Crossing to pouffe)* Morris—Joanna— Is this true?

GARRY. Of course it's true. It hasn't lasted quite so long as your rather dreary affair with Elvira Radcliffe—that's been hic-coughing along for nearly a year now.

JOANNA. Hugo!

(HUGO *turns up a step.)*

GARRY. And don't pretend that you didn't know, Joanna. You were absolutely delighted. It gave you room to expand.

(JOANNA *sits pouffe.)*

HUGO. How could you be so vile as to betray me? I told you about that in the deepest confidence.

GARRY. *(Crossing to Left)* I'm sick to death of being stuffed with everybody's confidences. I'm bulging with them. You all of you come to me over and over again and pour your damned tears and emotions and sentiment over me until I'm wet through. You're all just as badly behaved as I am really; in many ways a great deal worse. (HUGO *sits Center chair)* You believe in your amorous hangovers, whereas I at least have the grace to take mine lightly. *(Crosses back of sofa Up Center)* You wallow and I laugh, because I believe now and I always have believed that there's far too much nonsense talked about sex. (MORRIS *sits Up Right)* You, Morris, happen to like taking your paltry attachments seriously. You like suffering and plunging into orgies of jealousy and torturing yourself and everybody else. That's your way of enjoying yourself. Hugo's technique is a little different, he goes in for the domestic blend. That's why he got tired of Joanna so quickly. Anyhow he's beautifully suited with poor Elvira. She's been knee-deep in pasture ever since she left school. Joanna's different again. She devotes a great deal of time to sex, but not for any of the intrinsic pleasure of it, merely as a means to an end. She's a collector. An attractive, unscrupulous pirate. I personally am none of these things. To me the whole business is vastly overrated. I enjoy it for what it's worth and fully intend to go on doing so for as long as anybody's interested and when the time comes that they're not, I shall be perfectly content to go to bed with an apple and a good book! *(Crosses up on step.)*

MORRIS. Well, I'll be damned!

HUGO. Of all the brazen sophistry—

MORRIS. *(Rise)* You have the nerve to work yourself up into a state of moral indignation about us when we all know—

GARRY. I have not worked myself into anything at

all. I'm merely defending my right to speak the truth for once.

HUGO. *(Rises; crossing a step Center)* Truth! You wouldn't recognize the truth if you saw it. You spend your whole life attitudinizing and posturing and showing off.

GARRY. And I should like to know where we should all be if I didn't! I'm an artist, aren't I? Surely I may be allowed a little license!

MORRIS. As far as I'm concerned, it's expired.

(Men ad lib.)

LIZ. For heaven's sake stop shouting, all of you, you'll have the roof off.

HUGO. Listen, Garry, we're doing our best.

JOANNA. *(Rises; crossing to fire)* I'm sick of this idiotic performance.

MORRIS. Anyhow if it hadn't been for our restraining influence you'd be making B-pictures by now.

GARRY. I suppose you'll be saying next that it's your restraining influence that has allowed me to hold my position as the idol of the public for twenty years—

MORRIS. You're not the idol of the public.

GARRY. Oh! ! !

MORRIS. They'll come and see you in the right play and the right part and you've got to be good at that.

HUGO. If it hadn't been for us you'd have done "Peer Gynt."

(Pause.)

GARRY. If I so much as hear "Peer Gynt" mentioned in this house again I swear before heaven that I will have the most expensive production imaginable and produce it in the biggest theatre in London.

HUGO. Not on my money you won't! *(Crosses up by trunk.)*

GARRY. Oh, so we're back to that again, are we.

MORRIS. No, we're not back to anything. If it wasn't for the fact that Hugo and I signed the contract for the Forum Theatre this morning we should both of us wash our hands of you forever! *(Crosses Down Right.)*

GARRY. You've what! ! *(Crosses Down Right.)*

JOANNA. *(Crossing to trunk and gets purse and gloves. Loudly)* I'm going. Do you hear me, all of you? I'm going—for good.

LIZ. Take my car, it's downstairs.

JOANNA. It's been a great evening for speaking the truth, hasn't it, and I should like to add just one little contribution to the entertainment before I leave. I consider you, Mr. Garry Essendine, to be not only an overbearing, affected egomaniac, but the most unmitigated cad that it has ever been my misfortune to meet and I most devoutly hope that I shall never set eyes on you again as long as I live. (JOANNA *gives him a ringing slap on the face and picks up her bag and walks off.)*

GARRY. *(Not noticing it. Turns to* MORRIS) Do you mean to tell me that you signed a contract for that theatre, when I particularly told you that no power on God's earth would induce me to play in it?

HUGO. Now look here, Garry—

GARRY. *(Crossing to chair Center)* I will not look there. It's nothing more nor less than the most outrageous betrayal of faith, and I'm deeply, deeply angry— *(Sits chair Center.)*

MORRIS. *(Crossing to* GARRY) As I told you the other day they are doing up the whole theatre. They even consented to put a shower bath into your dressing room—

GARRY. I don't care whether they've put a swimming pool in my dressing room.

HUGO. It's going to be very comfortable.

LIZ. Darling, I've seen the designs—they're really awfully good.

GARRY. So you're against me too, are you. The whole world's against me.

MORRIS. Really, Garry, I promise you—

GARRY. *(Brokenly)* Go away—go away, all of you—I can't bear any more. I've got to face that dreadful sea voyage tomorrow and then those months of agonizing drudgery all across the length and breadth of what is admitted to be by everybody the most sinister continent there is. Go away from me—please go—

LIZ. *(Crossing to Left of* MORRIS*))* Go on, both of you. I'll talk to him.

MORRIS. That performance wouldn't deceive a kitten. He's losing his grip, Liz. Come on, Hugo.

HUGO. Peer Gynt!— Little Red Riding Hood's more like it.

(HUGO *and* MORRIS *go out front door.* LIZ *crosses to* GARRY.)

(WARN Curtain.)

GARRY. Who's that? Who's that? Oh— Liz. I think I should like a little sip of something. I really do feel quite tired.

LIZ. *(Crossing to bar)* Whiskey or brandy?

GARRY. Brandy, I think. It's more stimulating.

LIZ. All right. *(Crosses to* GARRY *with drink.)*

GARRY. *(Points to glass)* What's this?

LIZ. *(Sits Right arm of chair)* Brandy.

GARRY. Oh, yes. Brandy. It's more stimulating. You're not really coming to Africa with me, are you?

LIZ. Certainly I am. And not only to Africa. I'm coming back to you for good.

GARRY. I don't want you to come back to me. I'm perfectly happy as I am.

LIZ. That can't be helped. You behave abominably anyhow, but you won't be able to be quite so bad with me there.

GARRY. Liz, I implore you not to come back to me. Have you no sympathy? No heart?

LIZ. I'm thinking of the good of the firm. That reminds me, I must leave a note for Monica in the office.

I want her to ring up the bank for me first thing in the morning. *(Crosses to door Down Left.)*

GARRY. *(Rises. Putting glass down on table Center. Remembering)* The office! My God! *(Crosses to door Down Right then looks to Center.)*

LIZ. *(Crossing to* GARRY*)* What's the matter?

GARRY. *(In a hoarse whisper)* You've got a sofa, haven't you, in your flat?

LIZ. Of course. What are you talking about?

GARRY. You're not coming back to me, dear, I'm coming back to you!

(They tiptoe out to front door together as the)

CURTAIN FALLS. MEDIUM FAST.

PROPERTY PLOT

ACT ONE

Full Stage Carpet (Set according to Ground Plan)
Carpet or padding for Hall
Carpet or padding on stairs
Carpet or padding for off stage in bedroom
Curtains for windows
Drapes for windows. Flower row outside window
Pictures for walls
Fireplace Mantel with:
    Dressing—silver pitcher with ivy Down Right
        Clock Center. Head Left
    Ashtray
    Cigarette box with cigarettes
    Box of safety matches
                                        Right of clock
    1 double leather frame with photos of GARRY and
        LIZ, Left of clock
    Ashtray— Right of "Head"
Large Mirror hanging on wall above Mantel
    4 octagonal plaques— 2 on each side of mirror
Fireplace with:
    Set of andirons—Left
    Fire tender
    Large pan in fireplace to throw butts in for Act 3.
Large Pouffe, Right Center
Single chair below fireplace. (Has to be strong, without casters)
Sofa up stage Right
Table up stage Right against rail with:
    3 assorted books (important)
    Ashtray
    Leather easel picture frame with photo of GARRY

Large folding screen up Center on platform
Armchair front of screen— Left of table
Table front of screen with:
  Dressing— lamp—statuette
Bar on platform up Center with:
  Ashtray—1 or 2 butts—down stage
  4 sherry wine glasses—Left of highball glasses
  6 highball glasses—down stage
  2 whiskey glasses—Left of sherry glasses
  1 bottle of imported sherry wine—Left of Scotch (pinch bottle)
  1 bottle of Scotch whiskey—Left of brandy
  1 bottle of Martel brandy—Left stage
  2 siphon bottles of seltzer (practical)—1 empty—up stage
  1 white napkin
  Box of safety matches
  "Pink" flowers in vase
  1 bottle of gin—Left of Scotch
  3 bottles of Scotch (Left of gin)
Large sofa Left Center with:
  2 cushions (important)
Table Center with drawer, at Right of sofa with:
  Easel face mirror under table!!
  1 ashtray with butts in them
  Large cigarette box with cigarettes—to open up stage
  2 boxes of safety matches
  Under table—6 manuscripts, 2 books
Armchair Center
Table Left of sofa with:
  Dial hand telephone
  1 ash tray with butts
  Cigarette box with cigarettes
  2 boxes of safety matches
Grand piano up stage Left with:
  Dressing—lamp— up stage and
  Easel framed photo of MR. GARRY—front of lamp.
  Photo of LIZ.

Very large ashtray Right end
Schirmer Music book with maroon cover on music rack of piano
Vase of flowers at Right end (blue)
Piano bench front of piano.
Armchair below door Left.
Dressing for off stage in bedroom up stairs
Table; picture (statue) above it.

HAND PROPS

Off stage up Right in kitchen:
Dust cloth (ERIKSON)
Silent butler (ERIKSON)
Tray with:
Cup and saucer (coffee)
Spoon
Sugar bowl
Creamer
Small glass of orange juice
Napkins
Leg coffee table with:
Knife—fork—spoon
Silver covered dish of sliced bananas
Plate of Zwieback
Silver pot of coffee (with coffee)
Silver sugar bowl
Silver creamer
Cup—saucer—spoon—knife—fork—napkin.
Small tray with:
2 cups and saucers (coffee)
2 spoons
sugar
creamer
2 napkins

Off stage Right in hall:

String bag—in it 2 wrapped parcels (ERIKSON)

Cigarette case with cigarettes (HUGO)
Box of safety matches (HUGO)
Two dozen assorted letters stamped and sealed (MONICA)
Small ladies comb to fit in handbag (MONICA)
Box of fancy perfume (bottle sealed) for LIZ
White suitbox with man's dressing gown in it (get every performance from Mr. Horton) not wrapped
Small wrapped dummy express package (FRED)
Small wrapped dummy express package (ERIKSON)

Off stage Right in bedroom:

Handbag, hat and gloves (DAPHNE)

Off stage Left in office:

6 assorted loose letters (MONICA)
Stenographers notebook and pencil (MONICA)
1 ladies blue social letter with writing on it
1 postcard with scene—supposed to be from Brazil —stamped.

ACT TWO — SCENE I

Strike mirror—Strike piano bench—put chair from hall at piano
Set almost finished highball glass on piano
Strike all used sherry wine glasses
Strike siphon bottles
Set clean sherry wine glasses on bar
Strike tray with cups and saucers from table Left of sofa
Strike MONICA's hat—gloves and handbag
Strike dressing-gown box from piano
Strike perfume box
Strike 2 dozen stamped and sealed letters from off-stage Left and set off stage Right in hall

Strike torn postcard (get plenty of these as one is torn every performance)
Put cigarette box on table Left and 2 boxes of matches! ! !

Scene II

Put piano bench and chair back to original positions
Note: This change should be made as fast as possible.
Set chair from front of screen up on platform against rail Center
Put back in place single chair below fireplace
Strike cigarettes and highball glass from table Left of sofa
Strike ladies evening cape, bag, gloves from Center armchair
Strike all soiled highball glasses
Close lid and clear piano

Ready off stage Right in kitchen:

Silent butler (Erikson)
Dust cloth (Erikson)
Small tray with:
  Cup and saucer (coffee)
  Napkin
Letters—stamped and sealed—off Right— (Same as Act II)

ACT THREE

Set trunk against rail Center where chair had been
Set trunk up Right against Rail
Place ashtrays with butts on mantel
Express tags on all trunks and traveling bags
Set 2 English square cases Left of fire
Set 1 leather valise on chair in hall
Set 1 hatbox top of up Right trunk at fire

Set plate of soft cookies on table Right of sofa
Set below sofa, Right end, leg coffee table with:
  Silver covered dish of bananas (Same as Act I)
  Silver coffee pot with coffee (Same as Act I)
  Silver sugar bowl (Same as Act I)
  Silver creamer (Same as Act I)
  Plate of Zwieback
  Cup and saucer
  Knife, spoon, fork, napkin
Set waste basket by chair Center
Fill all ashtrays with butts
Be sure and check that large ashtray on piano is filled with butts and placed at Right end of piano
Strike and change all flowers
Strike tray with coffee cups and saucer from table Left of sofa
Place GARRY's coat on chair above fireplace
Set 24 open letters in armchair Center
Set 1 special typed blue social letter in armchair Center
Set Stenographer's notebook and pencil in armchair Center
Open piano
Check cigarette box full on Center table to open from Left
Check top of bottle on bar
Strike iris and put in blue on drink table Right
Tulips on piano
Strike hat under table Center
Strike gloves under table Center

Requirements:

Dressing room off stage Right with:
  mirror
  table chair
  hangers
Mirror off stage Left for GARRY
Chair and hangers
4 prop tables for off stage

Perishables:

Coffee—cigarettes
*Z*wieback—coca-cola
Bananas—toast
Sugar—soft cookies
Matches (safety)
Orange juice (1 glass)
2 siphon bottles

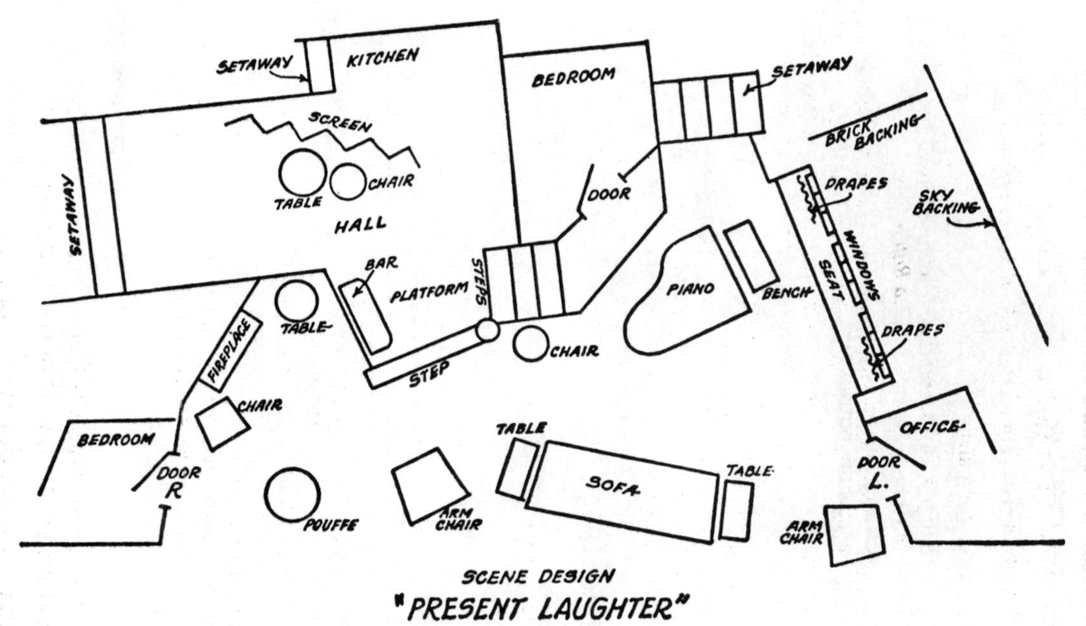

SCENE DESIGN
"PRESENT LAUGHTER"

The Lone Star Love Potion

MICHAEL PARKER

"Another hit for Parker."—*Palm Beach Post*

"Gales of laughter reached hurricane force. This play's a hoot."—*Boca Raton News*

Mr. Stancliff, the owner of a vast fortune and a 200,000-acre Texas ranch, has died. His unflappable butler, an alluring maid, the rancher's only living relative, her husband and the girl next door have gathered to hear the attorney read the will. Acting on the deceased's instructions, the butler produces a sample of what is reputed to be a potent love potion—with hilarious results. The flow of characters in, out and from under the beds reaches a frenetic pace before the truth about the potion is revealed. Anyone who savors uproarious farce, especially fans of the author's *The Amorous Ambassador* and *The Sensuous Senator,* is guaranteed to enjoy this original comedy. 3 m., 4 f. (#14209)

The Marriage Counselor

JOEY OUELLETTE

A traveling vacuum cleaner salesman wanders into a marriage counselor's office. Susan and Tiger burst in, arguing so fiercely that the salesman can't get a word in edge-wise. They mistake him for the marriage counselor and he never gets a chance to enlighten them. Next to arrive are Susan's sister (who is having an affair with Tiger) and a UPS man who is coincidentally Susan's lover. Things get even crazier when another UPS delivery person turns out to be Tiger's first wife who was presumed dead. That's when the man with the gun and a grudge storms in, determined to kill the counselor and everyone else if need be. When things get sorted out, three couples exit happily. 4 m., 3 f. (#15541)

Also available from Samuel French

POWER PLAYS

Elaine May and Alan Arkin

These one-act plays, *The Way of All Fish, Virtual Reality* and *In and Out of the Light,* were an Off-Broadway comedy sensation starring the authors. (#18234)

"Classic comedies ... with subversive details that keep catching you off guard.... The evening ... percolates with actorly inventiveness and a willingness to pursue a warped logic step by step into the land of absurdity. Has a heady sense of discovery, of seeing prototypical situations being twisted and spun to the point of dizziness, of disparate comic minds bouncing off each other."

The New York Times

"Hilarious as well as thoughtful."

New York Daily News

"A giddy delight."

New York Post

Act I of POWER PLAYS
The Way of All Fish by Elaine May

This power game is between a self-absorbed executive and her drab secretary. Over an impromptu dinner together, the executive's condescending graciousness drains away as the secretary explains her fantasy of gaining immortality by killing someone famous and successful — someone like her boss. 2 f. Int. (#24987)

"Oodles of laughs."
New York Daily News

Act II of POWER PLAYS
Virtual Reality by Alan Arkin

As two men wait for equipment to do an unspecified job, the one in charge insists on doing a dry-run inventory of the contents of the expected crates. The purely hypothetical assumes a wacky, sinister autonomy that transports them to a frozen, violent wilderness. 2 m. Int.

"A deeply funny, finely graded psychological portrait that becomes a tribute to the conjuring powers of theatre."
The New York Times

"Absurdist humor [like] Abbott and Costello lost in the *Twilight Zone.*"
New York Daily News

Act II of POWER PLAYS
In and Out of the Light by Elaine May

In this farcical delight, a workaholic dentist is attempting to have a fling with his curvaceous assistant. His plans are set hilariously awry by an after-hours patient who is a mega-neurotic psychologist with a pain-phobia and by a surprise visit from his son who has two heart-bursting announcements to make: he is gay (but celibate) and, worse, he doesn't want to be a dentist after all. 2 m., 2 f. Int. (#10990)

"Freewheeling ... farcical chaos ... with a surreal finale."
The New York Times